WHEN ELEPHANT WAS KING

WHEN ELEPHANT WAS KING

And other elephant tales from Africa

Told by Nick Greaves

Illustrated by Julie Bruton

SOUTHERN
BOOK PUBLISHERS

Dedicated to my wife, Steph

Acknowledgments

A great many people helped in the preparation of this book – some knowingly, some unwittingly.

For their advice and additional information I am indebted to Dr John Hutton, Mr Ron Thomson and the late Babs Thomson, Mr Ivan Ncube, Mr Kenneth Mwatongera, Mr Mike Jones, Dr Rosalie Osbourne, Mr Francis Odoom, Mr Hadebe, Bookie and Rich Peek, Scottie and Alan Elliott, Rod Clement, Will Travers and all at David Bateman Limited.

Special thanks go to the typist, Shirley Fenner, my son, Douglas, and especially to my wife, Steph.

Southern African edition.
This edition co-published in South Africa by
Southern Book Publishers
P.O. Box 3103, Halfway House
1685, South Africa
ISBN 186812 664 1

First published 1996
Reprinted 1999

© 1996 Nick Greaves – text
© 1996 David Bateman Ltd – art

This book is copyright. Except for the purpose of fair review, no part may be stored or transmitted in any form or by any means, electronic or mechanical, including recording or storage in any information retrieval system without permission in writing from the publisher. No reproduction may be made, whether by photocopying or by any other means, unless a licence has been obtained from the publisher or its agent.

A David Bateman Book
Designed by Errol McLeary
Typeset by TTS Jazz, Auckland
Printed in Hong Kong by Everbest Printing Co

Contents

"Were there no elephants in the jungle, then the buffalo would be large."

An Efe saying

Introduction

The African elephant once roamed the vast continent of Africa from the northern coastal fringes of the Mediterranean along the Valley of the Nile, and south of the vast Sahara Desert down to the Cape of Good Hope. Vast herds of these magnificent beasts roamed the interior at will. From high mountain pastures to coastal mangrove swamps, through dense tropical jungle to open grasslands and savannah, even in the harsh, arid semi-deserts of the Sahel and Kalahari, the elephant roamed unhindered.

Sadly, the concentration and diversity of wild animals in this part of the world is a thing of the past. As Africa was developed by the colonial powers of Western Europe, the endless herds and wide open plains were pushed further into the interior. The Voortrekkers, the ivory hunters and eventually the farmers that followed in their wake, started a slaughter so complete that in many areas the indigenous animals were exterminated. Some species, such as the Cape lion, bloubok and quagga, were driven into extinction, never to be seen again.

The elephant has been driven from its natural range which spanned the vast continent and now lives mostly in areas of sanctuary and protection. These form a fragmented network of isolated reserves and havens, hopefully protected from the ever-growing demands of land hungry people. The development of Africa has been a story of the decimation of the elephant.

Since the dawn of human history, our cave-dwelling ancestors coveted ivory and carved religious artifacts and trinkets from this beautiful and precious material. With the advent of the slave trade the Arab, Portuguese and European colonists and slavers increased the profitability of this enterprise by ensuring that each healthy slave carried an elephant tusk from the interior to the coast. The cost in suffering and misery was borne by both humans and animals alike!

After the slave trade was abolished in the middle of the last century, the ivory trade not only continued, but increased in intensity. The relentless onslaught against the elephant continued unabated to supply the world's growing population with everything from jewelery to billiard balls, Hanko seals (Japanese carved ivory signature stamps) to statues and even piano keys. This uncontrolled exploitation was thought to be in check by the 1960s, but while measures of protection were being implemented and becoming effective, the demand for ivory had not lessened. What creature has a chance for a future in the face of such greed?

The most cataclysmic decline in the elephant population took place in the decade between 1979 and 1989. In 1979 the African elephant population was estimated to be over 1.3 million animals. It took only ten years of intensive and bloody poaching to reduce the population to 660,000. In many areas the bulls carrying massive tusks were the first to go, followed by the matriarchs and the mothers – even babies with only a couple of inches of ivory were gunned down in order to recover their precious teeth.

In many areas where they previously lived, the elephant is now only a memory. In others, delinquent groups of infant and teenager animals try to piece together the fabric of family life without parents and guardians. Their chances of survival are limited by their lack of knowledge of when and where to find food and water in times of hardship as they have been deprived of the herd's collective memories which are passed down from generation to generation.

The slaughter of the ivory poachers was so intense that in 1989 a special meeting of CITES (Convention on International Trade in Endangered Species) was called. At this meeting the African elephant was given the highest level of protection and an international ban was placed on the trade in elephant products and ivory. This desperate measure came just in time; the price and demand for ivory literally died away overnight and within a year very few elephants fell to the poacher's gun. The shell-shocked remnant population was given a chance for the future.

This hope for the future could be taken away from the elephant if the next CITES meeting in Harare, in 1997, allows the South African Government to resume trading in ivory. Other Governments in Southern Africa, such as Zimbabwe and Botswana, will no doubt also resume trading if given the chance. Though Southern Africa was least affected by the poaching holocaust of the 1980s, huge tonnages of illegal ivory were routed through the area. The greed and corruption that has been dormant since the 1989 ban, lies waiting to be resurrected.

Let us hope that there is still a future for the African elephant, the world's largest living land mammal, and that human greed and ignorance does not drive this spectacular giant over the dark abyss of extinction, as our cave dwelling ancestors drove the woolly mammoth, a cousin of the elephant, into extinction several thousand years ago.

Extinction is forever. Besides, ivory really does look best on the elephant!

The Bantu Peoples

Two thousand years ago, the Roman Empire was finally established after Rome's third and final war against Carthage. But the Roman army's movement south was curtailed by the vast Sahara Desert. As the Emperor Augustus consolidated the boundaries in Europe, the Middle East, and Northern Africa, the Bantu people of sub-Saharan Africa set out on their own massive wave of expansion and development, covering major parts of the African continent.

The Bantu people originated in western Central Africa in the region of modern day Cameroon. At this time, eastern and southern Africa was inhabited by the stone age cultures of the San peoples and the Pygmies, or Efe, in the central rain forests. Small family groups of San roamed vast areas of the region, living in close harmony with nature and the animal inhabitants of the bush. They were hunter-gatherers and led a nomadic life.

The Bantu people from West Africa quickly spread across the center of the continent. They opened up the northern part of the Zaire basin and the headwaters of the White Nile in the fertile lands of the western Rift Valley and the Lake Victoria region. The new settlers further developed their skills in crop production and animal husbandry and, above all, the art of working metals – a technological advancement against which the stone age San could not compete.

The diminutive Efe of the equatorial rain forests learned to live with the Bantu and, to a large extent, became assimilated into the Bantu culture. The

San did not fare so well and they were gradually pushed off most of their traditional lands, eventually retaining only the harsh, dry Kalahari Desert, which was not sought after by the new agriculturalists and livestock herders. The San retained their language of peculiar clicks and shunned contact with the Bantu, maintaining their ethnic identity even today.

The expansion of the Bantu was not one of imperialism, but rather a process of demographic development. Their new technologies supported ever-growing populations and their remorseless southward movement was in search of new lands to develop and expand. This expansion eventually brought them into contact with the northward expansion of the European colonies in the Cape.

Today's widely dispersed tribal groups within Southern Africa all stem from a common ancestry. The history of the Bantu was not recorded by the written word, but rather by word of mouth. Storytellers related the history and development of the migrations, and over the millennia the myths and legends of Southern Africa have a remarkable similarity between tribes widely dispersed across the sub-continent and with outwardly differing cultures.

Facts about Elephants

The African Elephant is divided into two distinct sub-species, the larger bush elephant (*Loxodonta africana*) and the smaller forest elephant (*Loxodonta africana cyclotis*). All references in this book are to the better known and more widely spread bush elephant though, of course, the stories from the tribal groups that live in equatorial forest regions, such as the Pygmy and Efik, refer to the forest elephant.

The distribution of the forest elephant, as shown on Map I (page 11), corresponds very closely to the equatorial forest zone as shown in Map 4 (page 17). The forest elephant has adapted and evolved to life in the dense jungle where its small size no doubt makes feeding and movement much easier in the dense undergrowth. The larger bush elephant, on the other

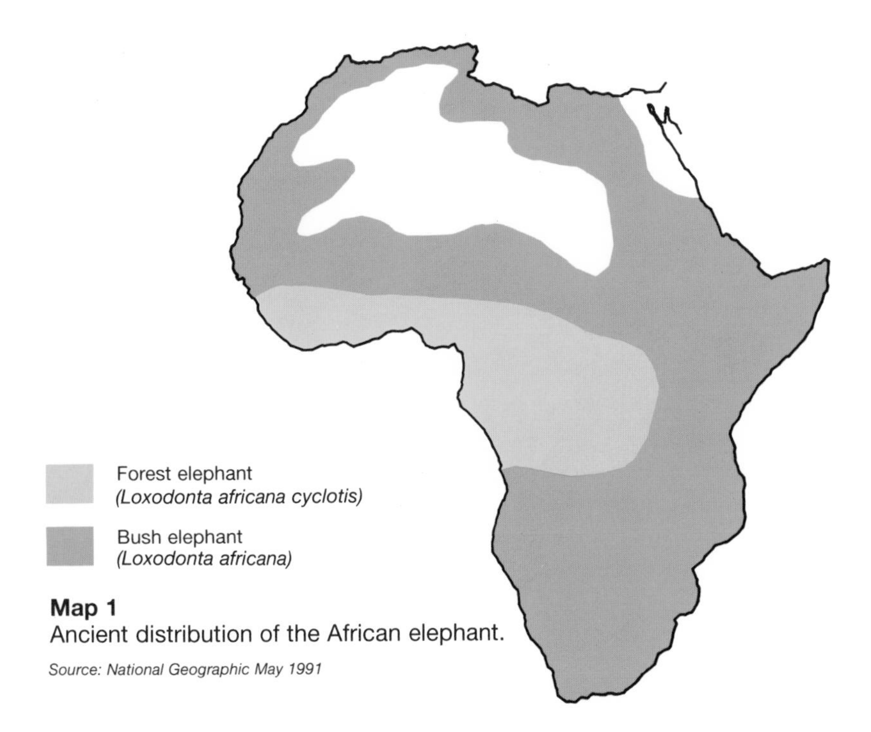

Map 1
Ancient distribution of the African elephant.
Source: National Geographic May 1991

hand, is far wider spread and has adapted to eating a wider range of vegetation as found in the varying dominant plant species in the other zones. In ancient times the only area that was not inhabited by elephants was the barren and waterless Sahara Desert.

The elephant, like most of the larger species of African wildlife, is now confined to National Parks and ever-diminishing areas of wilderness. These areas are carefully managed to ensure that a healthy environment is maintained for all members of the animal and plant community. Some large species, such as elephant and buffalo, must at times be culled to prevent their numbers rising above an area's ability to maintain a state of balance.

In 1992 and 1993 Zimbabwe successfully captured and relocated adult elephants to areas where they had been wiped out. Up until these recent pioneering capture operations, it was considered impossible to relocate adult elephants and this opens up exciting new possibilities for restocking areas in the rest of Africa where populations have been decimated by ivory poachers. This offers a far more humane, though expensive alternative, to

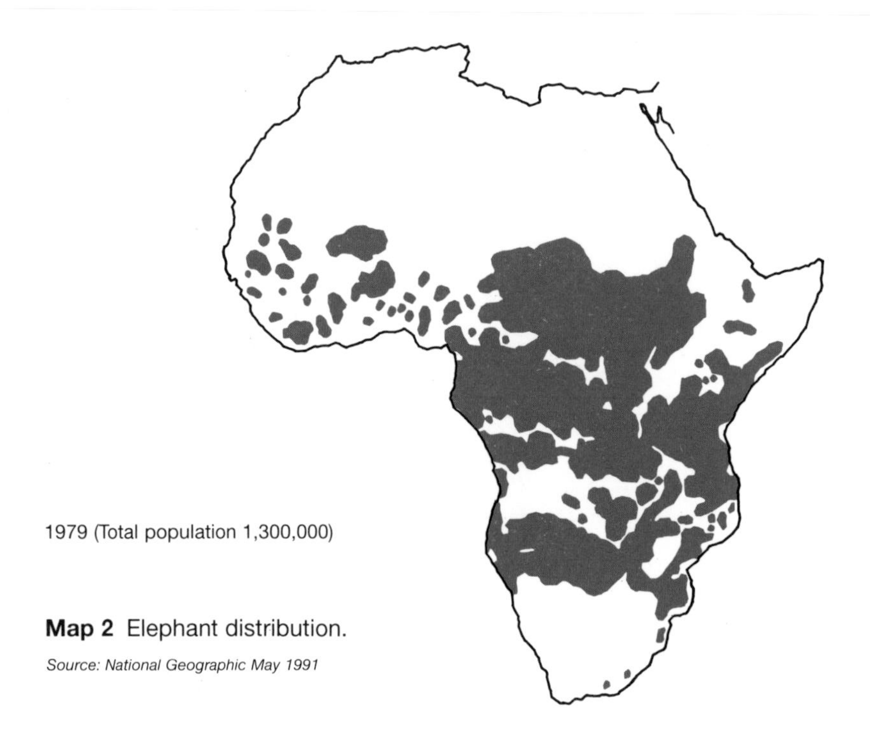

Map 2 Elephant distribution.
Source: National Geographic May 1991

culling these magnificent, intelligent beasts and one that will benefit the tourist industries and economies of many African countries.

An interesting fact is that the African elephant's ear is the same shape as the outline of Africa. Its smaller cousin and only living relative, the Indian elephant, has a smaller ear and this is similar to the outline of the Indian subcontinent. Unlike the Indian elephant, which has been tamed and trained to work for many centuries, very few attempts have been made to tame the African elephant. One man who did was Hannibal, the Carthaginian general who used elephants in his wars against the Roman Empire, even crossing the European Alps with them in an ill-fated, surprise attack on Rome in the year 219 B.C. Hannibal was a gifted general who used his trained elephants as living tanks and won many spectacular victories over the might of Imperial Rome.

Since these ancient times, the only serious attempt to train the African elephant was made in the former colony of the Belgian Congo, now Zaire,

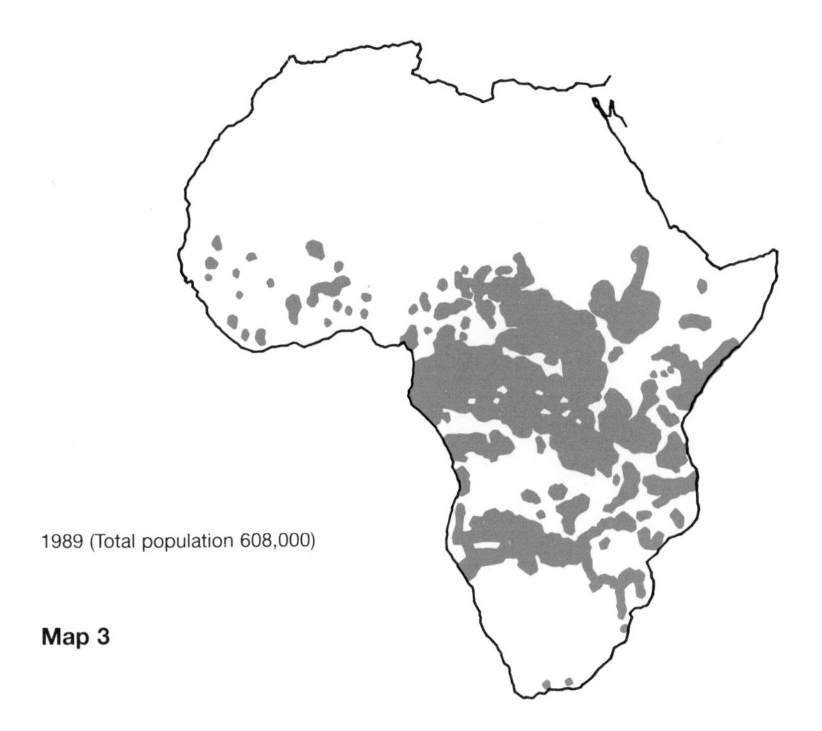

1989 (Total population 608,000)

Map 3

where forest elephants were trained for more peaceful duties such as logging operations and bush clearing. For nearly fifty years hundreds of elephants were trained to help people, but on gaining independence the programme fell into disuse. An exciting new attempt has been launched in Botswana where a safari company offers the opportunity of riding in Indian style howdahs on the back of an African elephant through the beautiful Okavango Swamps. This is an exciting and unique way of viewing game, who accept the elephant as part of the natural scenery. Elephant safaris are also available in Zimbabwe.

Human beings and the African elephant both evolved over millions of years on the African continent. But as human population grows, it seems to be at the expense of the wilderness. We can only hope that people will have the compassion and the common sense to protect and leave intact the few remaining areas of wilderness so that future generations can witness and enjoy the magnificent elephant, the "Grey Ghost of Africa."

The Elephant Species

AFRICAN ELEPHANT *(Loxodonta africana)*

	Male	**Female**
Height at shoulder	10 ft (3 m)	9 ft (2.75 m)
Weight	11,000 lbs (4,980 kg)	7,700 lbs (3,490 kg)
Weight at birth	264 lbs (120 kg)	264 lbs (120 kg)
Age at weaning	2 years	2 years
Gestation period	—	22 months
Number of young	—	1
Life-span	60 years	60 years

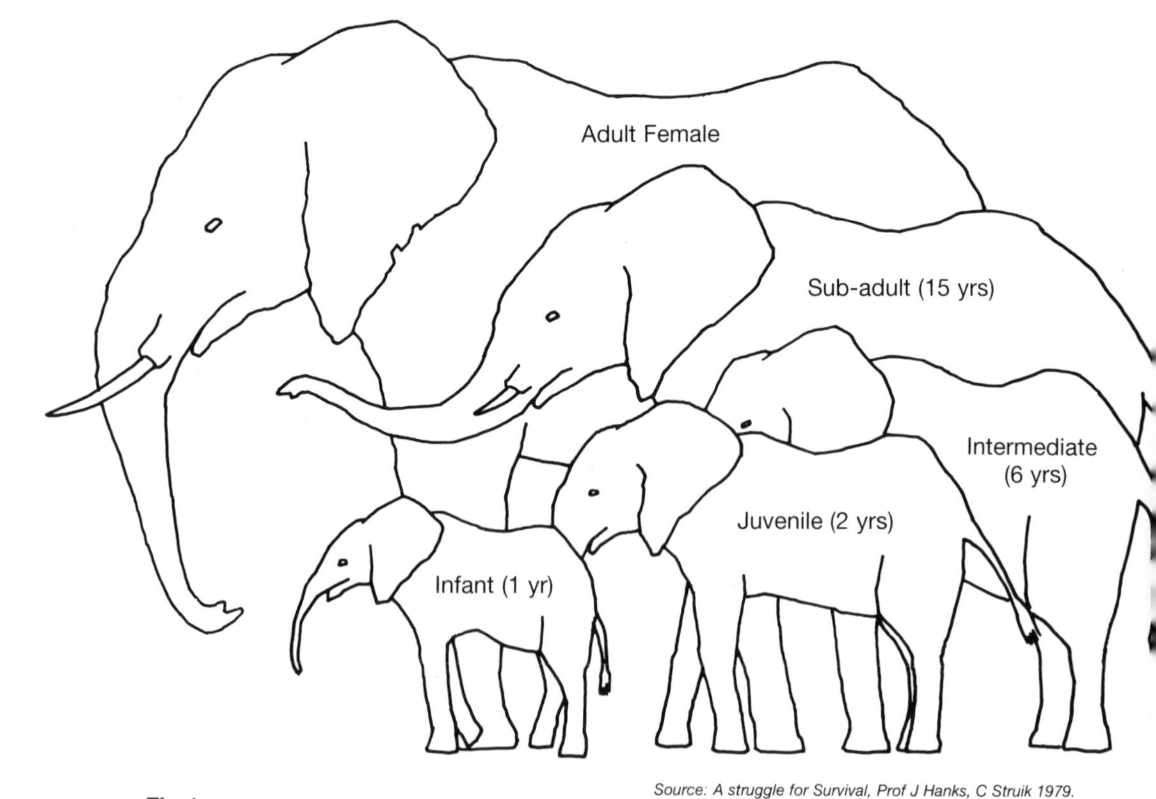

Source: A struggle for Survival, Prof J Hanks, C Struik 1979.

Fig 1
A useful field guide for the comparison of age to the relative size of elephants in a family unit compared with that of an average lead cow or matriarch.

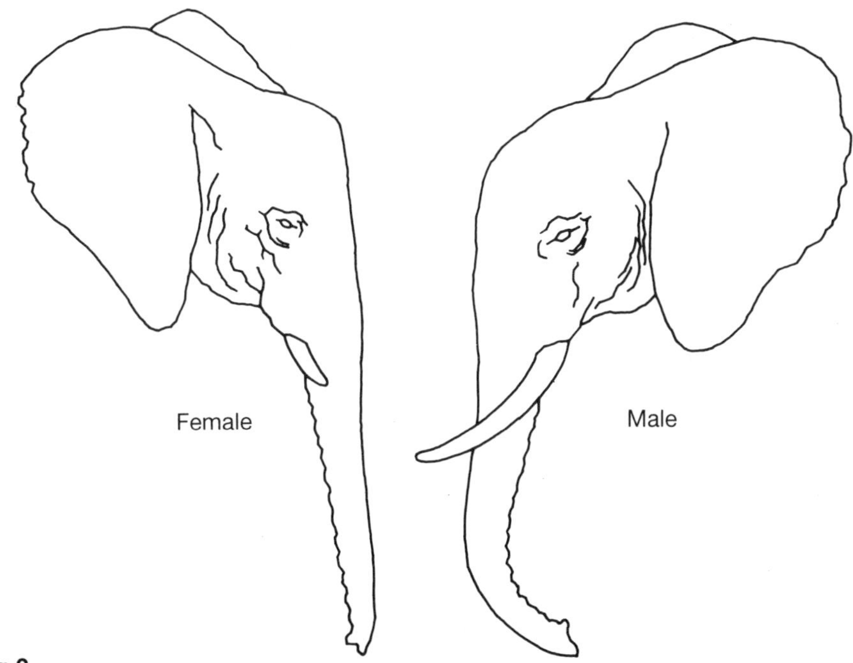

Fig 2
A comparison of the profile shape of the forehead in male and female elephants, another useful field guide in determining age and sex.

Adult bulls are often solitary or form loosely associated bachelor groups.

Females live in family groups, daughters normally remaining in their mother's family group for life. The family unit is the core of elephant society and closely related females form larger herds from time to time. These temporary herd gatherings can number up to 200 animals.

The elephant's only real enemy is people who hunt them for their meat and especially their ivory, which are actually specially adapted incisor teeth. Tough scavengers and predators, such as lions, will eat off the carcass of a dead elephant. Adults do not fear predation, but mothers are highly protective of their young which, if they got lost, could be killed or preyed upon by lions or hyenas.

Adult males are usually much larger than females with bigger, thicker tusks. It is easy to tell the difference between the sexes as males have broader, domed foreheads, while the female's forehead is more angular – see Figure 2.

Figure 1 shows a useful way of comparing the size of an elephant to other members of the group and assessing its age. Infants up to one-year-old are small enough to walk under their mother's belly. A six-year-old is normally about half the size of an adult female.

Elephants are born with six sets of teeth, but only one set is in use at a time. As these molars become worn, the next set grow forward to replace them. As the last set of teeth wear down, the animal is no longer able to chew its food properly and will slowly starve. With the wear rate of their teeth, elephants can only live to a maximum age of about sixty years.

Tooth	Age in years
M1	1
M2	2
M3	6
M4	15
M5	28
M6	47

Identification

Being the largest land mammal, identification of the African elephant should cause no problems. Their massive size, huge bodies, stout legs, large ears, and long trunks make the elephant unique among animals.

Their loose fitting skin is a dark gray in color and, at times, the elephant may appear white or even red after a dust bath or mud wallow. An elephant does not have skin pores as an animal its size would lose too much water if it sweated. To regulate body temperature an elephant's ears are densely packed with blood vessels which act in a similar manner to a car radiator. When an elephant flaps its ears it is, in fact, cooling itself down. Cooling baths also help the animal to get rid of excess body heat.

Tusk size can vary greatly, bulls usually having larger and thicker tusks than the cows. Many elephants break their tusks during their lives as they constantly use them to dig up mineral salts and to gouge tree trunks to strip off bark to eat. Most elephants have one tusk that they use more than the other and, as a result, one gets more worn down. Some elephants have no tusks at all and are usually considered more ill-tempered than those with tusks.

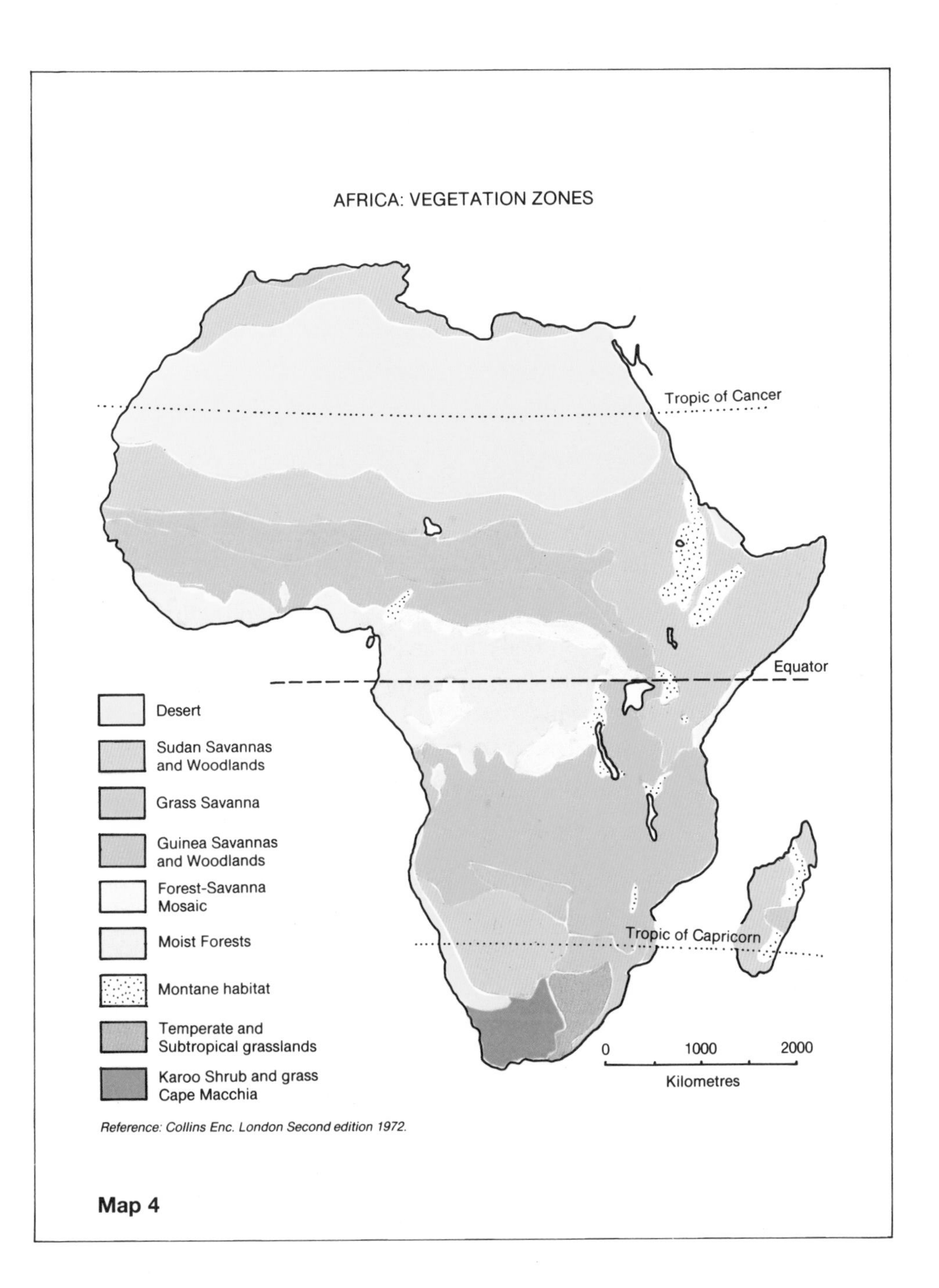
AFRICA: VEGETATION ZONES
Tropic of Cancer
Equator
Tropic of Capricorn
Desert
Sudan Savannas and Woodlands
Grass Savanna
Guinea Savannas and Woodlands
Forest-Savanna Mosaic
Moist Forests
Montane habitat
Temperate and Subtropical grasslands
Karoo Shrub and grass Cape Macchia
0
1000
2000
Kilometres
Reference: Collins Enc. London Second edition 1972.

Map 4

Habitat

Elephants can be found in a wide range of habitats ranging from grassy, open woodland to dense forests, and even high up on mountains. This is possible because of the variety of vegetation an elephant can eat.

Elephants are capable of undertaking large scale migrations when seasonal variation in food and water supply demand, and they can cross rivers, lakes, and mountain ranges. However, these are now a thing of the past as human encroachment on the few remaining areas of wilderness have confined elephants to reserves and sanctuaries.

Habits

The elephant is a highly social animal and lives in well-structured family groups varying in size from two to twenty animals. These family groups are ruled by a mature female called the matriarch. Most of the day-to-day decisions on when and where to feed or drink are decided by the matriarch, whose years of experience tell her what seasonal food sources are ripe and ready to eat. The younger animals in the family group learn by example from their elders and the collective knowledge of a herd can span many generations.

While daughters normally remain with their mother's family group, young males usually leave the breed herd when they are adolescents of about twelve to fourteen years of age. These young bulls either live solitary lives or form loosely associated "bachelor" herds, youngsters learning from the mature bulls, but free to go their own way at will.

Elephants can congregate into large herds in times of drought or when subjected to heavy poaching pressure, and herds of up to 200 animals have been recorded. The large herds are really temporary associations of many family groups and are often inter-related.

Elephants love water and are excellent swimmers. They will normally drink every day when water is readily available, but can go up to three or four days between drinks in hard times. A large bull can drink over 53 gallons (200 liters) at a time by filling his trunk with water and then squirting it down his throat. Young elephants that have not yet mastered the use of

their trunks can be seen kneeling at the water's edge and drinking with their mouths.

After drinking, elephants spend long periods bathing and wallowing in the mud and this is obviously a time of play and enjoyment for them all, no matter how old! Their activities at water holes and the mud they carry off on their hides helps create and develop many pans and water holes.

It has only recently been discovered that elephants communicate with each other not only in close proximity by touch, gesture, or loud rumblings and squeals, but also over long distances. Elephants utilize low frequency sound, known as infrasound, which carries over long distances and is below the human range of hearing. Infrasound enables herds to keep in contact over a large area and is a useful means of warning. Scientists were mystified as to how elephants could act in unison, even when they were scattered over large areas and unable to see each other, until the secret of infrasound was discovered.

The elephant also has an excellent sense of smell and, again, this is assisted by its trunk. The trunk is actually a fusion of the nose and upper lip which evolved over the last sixty million years. Elephants are often seen raising their trunks to smell the breeze and this helps them detect other elephants and also possible danger long before they can see it. The trunk contains thousands of muscles and is sensitive enough to pick up objects as small as berries, yet strong enough to tear down branches. It is also an excellent snorkel and helps the animal to breathe when swimming.

Diet

Elephants both graze and browse, eating a wide variety of leaves, flowers, fruit, roots, tree bark, and grass. During the rainy season, when the grass is at its most succulent and nutritious, it forms the basis of the elephant's diet. As the dry season progresses the diet changes to include more leaves, tree bark, and roots.

A large bull elephant can eat up to 660 lb (300 kg) of food in a day, while females eat about 440 lb (200 kg). The elephant's trunk plays an essential part in harvesting such a large diet. Whether reaping clumps of grass, or picking up berries one by one, these acts would be impossible without a trunk. During the dry season the elephant uses its trunk to tear down branches that would otherwise be beyond its reach.

Because of its huge size and bulk, an elephant is capable of pushing over large trees to get at their foliage. It also uses its tusks to gouge and loosen tree bark which it then strips off with its trunk. It also digs into the moist, pulpy cores of trees such as the baobab which can cause the tree to die or collapse.

Many consider the elephant to be a wasteful feeder because of the damage it does to trees, but many trees will produce new shoots. This action by the vegetation, or flora, allows many other animals to utilize this food source that otherwise would not have been made available to them had it not been for the elephant's 'destructive' feeding habits.

As the elephant has to spend most of the day feeding to obtain enough food, it is forced to be active by day and by night and it often feeds during the night. Such a large proportion of its time is spent on the move that the elephant has to snatch quick 'cat naps' and snooze at irregular intervals.

Breeding

The elephant has the longest gestation period of any mammal, taking twenty two months. Mating normally occurs during the rainy season when the more nutritious diet brings most of the females that do not already have infants, into season. This ensures that the young are born during the rainy season, two years later. This is not always the case, though birth is predominantly during the rains.

Until recently it was not known that 'musth' occurred in the African elephant, as it has been known to do in its Indian cousin for centuries. Musth is the name for the seasonal peak in a male's readiness for breeding. It is signalled by a noticeable discharge from a gland in the animal's temple and a noticeable increase in aggressiveness. Musth can occur at any time of the year, but is more common during the rainy season and occurs at the same time of year in an individual animal.

When a female comes into season she is accompanied by a dominant bull, usually one in musth, for a period of three days or so when mating takes place. The dominant musth bull will fight with any other bull that tries to take over as her consort. Serious injury is usually avoided as most bulls in an area know each other and have already established their dominance hierarchy. Serious injury and, on occasion, death, can result if such a fight is allowed to develop.

When a cow is ready to give birth she usually moves away from the herd, but is often accompanied by the matriarch and one or two close female relatives. The birth is usually announced by a great deal of excitement and general ruckus, but the mother, helped by the matriarch, will normally keep curious well-wishers at a distance for a couple of hours. The calf learns to suckle quickly and is assisted by the mother to find her breasts. These are situated between her front legs, which is unusual in most four-legged animals. The calf suckles with its mouth, curling the trunk up and to one side so that it does not get in the way.

The calf will usually suckle for the first two years before being weaned. The youngster will start eating solid foods after a couple of months, learning what to eat from its mother.

The young grow up in a caring, loving family group and will be protected and cared for by all in the group. As with humans, it is in the childhood years that an elephant learns all that it needs to know in later life.

Tribal Beliefs and Superstitions About Elephants

The elephant is greatly respected by the tribal people of Africa for its size and dignity, as well as its potential danger to humans.

The Karanga, a group of the Shona speaking people of Zimbabwe, make a distinction between two types of elephant – Goronga the tusker with its magnificent ivory, and Muri, the tuskless one.

Muri, though unarmed, is often the stronger of the two and certainly the more cantankerous. The Karanga believe that should Goronga and Muri fight, then Muri will uproot a sapling, or pick up a log with which to beat his opponent. Muri is also believed to associate more closely with the herds of females and therefore sires more young than the tuskers, who normally lure a cow away from the herd to mate.

The Shona also speak of the 'wisdom sticks' that elephants often have embedded in their temporal glands on either side of their heads. They believe that these wisdom sticks enable the animal to foresee the future and the time and place of their deaths. That is why they say an old tusker, Goronga, is seen wandering the bush alone instead of concealing his ivory in the safety of the herd. He knows his time is near and he wishes to die alone, in peace.

Many tribes believe that elephants know that people covet their beautiful ivory and that an animal will do its best to prevent the hunter from getting his tusks. Sometimes they deliberately break their tusks in the forks of trees, or smash them on rocks.

All tribes have various superstitions about hunting elephants. Before going on a hunt, none of the men participating can sleep with their wives, or other women. The elephant is believed to know everything, both good and bad. Any transgressor would be given short shrift and bring disaster on himself and his companions. Tuskless bulls and cows are supposed to charge and kill anyone guilty of adultery unless they immediately confess their guilt to the elephant.

A hunter who sets out nursing a grievance may wound his prey and not get a kill. If he meets an elephant with his trunk curled around his head, he knows some tragedy has struck at home. Should he see an elephant flinging earth over its back, it means that his wife is bathing, which she is not supposed to do while he is out hunting.

The chief of the area is often entitled to the tusk beneath the fallen elephant, even though it may be broken. Apart from the valuable ivory and meat, the hunters also prize the wisdom sticks. They remove them after killing an elephant, grind them to a powder, boil the powder with herbs and lion fat, and then swallow the mixture. This is supposed to induce dreams about elephants and the hunter may be confident of a successful hunt the next day.

The Shona also believe that the elephant swallows a pebble each year to keep count of its age. They also believe that elephant's main enemies are rhino, warthog, lion, leopard and crocodile while buffalo is elephant's friend.

Many tribes have various uses for elephant parts that are deeply rooted in the history of tribal folklore. Ngangas, or medicine men, have long used elephant bile stones, kidney and intestinal fat, ivory pearls, and tusk buds for medicinal and magical purposes. The ivory, ground to powder and mixed with certain potions, is said to cure acne, and tusk buds may be used to remove cataracts. Dried and powdered trunk tip is an important ingredient in the magic horn worn by some hunters to protect them in case of an attack by an elephant. The fat from the heart is thought by some to be valuable for ensuring conception, and by others to be a valuable additive to the daily food eaten by men.

The wearing of a bracelet of elephant hair not only confers status on the wearer, providing he personally slew the elephant from which the hair was taken, but is said to act as a protective charm against attacking elephants. Many other parts of the elephant's body are used for specific purposes by particular tribes around Africa.

The degree of respect that many tribes had for elephant is reflected in the terms of praise for great chiefs and warriors, such as Shaka Zulu, whose ultimate accolade was that of "Oh Great Mighty Elephant of the Zulu!" while his mother, Nandi, was praised as "The Mighty She-Elephant!"

Elephants assumed the peak of power and wisdom that humans can attain.

When Elephant was King

(A Shona legend)

At the beginning of time, before people lived on the earth, all the animals of the bush lived together under one king. That king was Elephant.

King Elephant was fair to his subjects. He was able to maintain his authority without too much grumbling from them. There were, of course, several characters on whom Elephant had to keep a close eye. Hare was one of these. His mischievous nature had to be carefully watched. But it was Lion who was Elephant's main rival for the position of king.

Lion made all kinds of attempts to become king, but no one took his efforts seriously. They all knew that it was Elephant who possessed all the qualities of genuine leadership.

One year disaster struck. The rains failed and the animals soon ran short of water. One by one, the water holes began to dry up and their plight became very serious. Such was their distress that King Elephant called a council of all the animals where they were all invited to come up with suggestions.

Even Hare had something to say and, as the situation was so desperate, he was allowed to approach the platform and speak. Everyone was so eager to find a solution that thousands of pairs of eyes silently watched him, many having forgotten Hare's disreputable character.

"Ladies and Gentlemen," Hare began, "I wish to officially offer my solution to our terrible problem. My solution is one that will allow us all to survive these thirsty nights. I suggest that everyone bites his or her own wrist so that we can all drink the blood left within our own bodies...."

The sentence went unfinished as the angry crowd pelted Hare with sticks and stones. This was without doubt one of the stupidest of Hare's devious tricks and some of the animals even chased him into the bush.

King Elephant decided that their short-term solution to the lack of drinking water was to dig a large, new well in the nearby river bed. The water table had dropped drastically and the animals had to work day and night without resting. King Elephant worked hardest of all using his enormous tusks to dig

deep into the river bed, while the others carried away the soil, mouthful by mouthful.

Eventually Elephant reached water and the animals rejoiced, praising the strength and hard work of their wise king. Then Elephant made rules about the water hole so that the water should be shared equally and everyone could quench their thirst. He decided that the animals could only come and drink at sunrise and sunset.

Lion was jealous of all the praise the other animals gave Elephant. He devised a plan to destroy Elephant's image and become king in his place. After all the animals had agreed to Elephant's drinking schedule, they went off for a well earned sleep. In the dead of night Lion crept down to the well and drank his fill.

After he had drunk his fill, Lion had a bath and muddied up the water. He then gathered up some mud which he carried to the sleeping Elephant and smeared over his feet. Elephant did not wake up but continued to sleep soundly, tired from his labors.

However, Lion's plan was neither well thought out, or cleverly executed. The next morning the animals discovered the muddy water hole and were very angry. Who could be so thoughtless as to disobey the King's orders and ruin the precious water hole? When everyone gathered together it soon

became clear that Lion was one of the culprits – he had forgotten to clean the mud from his coat and paws.

But Lion, who was still determined to implicate Elephant and make him lose face with his subjects, pointed to Elephant's muddy feet. The animals stared aghast, not wanting to believe their king might also have deceived them.

Elephant was not worried by the accusation. He told Hyena to check around the pool and see whose spoor was left as evidence in the soft mud. Hyena obeyed and was soon back to tell everyone that Lion's was the only fresh spoor at the water hole.

"See, I do not fly, so how could I have been at the water hole?" exclaimed Elephant. All the animals now saw through Lion's plan and in rage they banished him from Elephant's kingdom. King Elephant won back the trust of his subjects and reigned over them for a long time. The rains returned soon after and life was good.

By the time the old elephant died many years later, he was the most respected animal in the land. Lion now had his chance and proclaimed himself to be King of the Beasts. After his takeover many things changed and the animals of the bush were no longer ruled by a fair and just leader. There was much grumbling and you would often overhear statements such as, "If only things were like they used to be, when Elephant was King!"

"An elephant never forgets."

A common saying

Why Elephant has a Trunk

This traditional tale is common to several tribal groups in Southern Africa, such as the Venda of the Northern Transvaal and the Shangaan of the Transvaal and Zimbabwe. The tale obviously formed the basis of the story made famous by Rudyard Kipling in his "Just So" stories, which he wrote after his visiting the region during the Second Boer War.

In the beginning of time, the Creator brought forth all the animals of the bush and birds and insects of the air from the roots of a huge baobab tree. Most of the creatures look the same as they did then, but some have changed in appearance since the time of Creation.

One such animal is Elephant, who originally did not possess a trunk but a pig-like snout instead. Feeding was a constant problem for such a large, thick-set animal and it seemed that Elephant had to eat non-stop morning, noon and night to satisfy the needs of his enormous body. Drinking was even

more complicated as Elephant had to kneel at the water hole and gulp down great mouthfuls of water to quench his thirst. Both eating and drinking were laborious and time-consuming.

One day a group of elephants trekked a long way from their feeding grounds to a distant water hole – the long dry season had dried up most of the smaller pans and springs. This water hole was the home of a huge, old crocodile who had gone without food for a long time and was feeling particularly hungry on that day.

When Crocodile saw the herd approaching, he slipped quietly from the sandbank, where he had been sunning himself, into the murky water. Swimming slowly along, with just his eyes and nostrils showing above the surface, Crocodile cruised over to where he knew the elephants would drink, without making a ripple on the pool's smooth surface. Not even the inquisitive vervet monkey, feeding high in the nearby trees, saw him swim to where he now lay in ambush.

The elephants made their way down the well trodden game trail to the sandy beach. There they laboriously sank to their knees and started to gulp down the refreshing water. Crocodile saw his opportunity, and with a huge splash he lunged with terrifying speed at the young bull elephant drinking closest to him.

The other elephants lumbered to their feet, squealing in fright, and turned to run away. All, that is, but the young bull, who had Crocodile's vice-like jaws clamped over his pig-like snout. A terrible tug-of-war then started. Try as they might, the other elephants could not get a decent hold on the young bull to help set him free. Crocodile used all his great strength and weight to try to pull the young bull elephant into the water. Elephant was also strong and heavy, and despite the pain in his snout, he used his great strength and weight to save himself.

For hours both these great creatures pulled and tugged in their desperate battle, and bit by bit the only thing that gave way was Elephant's snout. With each pull and tug Elephant's nose stretched a little. On and on went the battle and more and more was Elephant's nose stretched until eventually Crocodile's energy was spent. Exhausted after hours and hours of pulling and tugging, Crocodile suddenly let go of Elephant's nose and slid back into the quiet pool. So sudden was his release that Elephant sprawled back in the sand, surprised by Crocodile's surrender.

The other elephants gathered round, relieved at the young bull's escape. But when they realised that he was not badly hurt, they started to laugh at him. The young bull was mortified by this, especially as his poor, torn nose was very tender and painful. When he looked at his reflection in a shallow pool nearby, however, he had to admit he was the strangest looking elephant he had ever seen!

Instead of a short snout he now had a long, rubbery trunk that stretched down to the ground. No matter what he did, he could not get it to shrink back to its normal size and he had to suffer further jeers and taunts from the other elephants.

As time went by the wounds healed and the pain subsided, but he was still left with an embarrassingly wobbly, useless trunk. He spent more and more time on his own, away from the herd. Eventually he came to terms with the fact that he was stuck with his strange new appendage. Slowly, but surely, he learned how to control his trunk and to put it to use.

He learned how to use it to make feeding and drinking much quicker and easier, allowing him more time for relaxation. The trunk was most useful in enabling him to cross rivers that were deeper than head height, and to scent breezes to check for danger, or other elephants. He could now pull down the most succulent fruits and leaves from the highest branches, uproot the tenderest grasses, and pop them all in his mouth! He could even pick up sticks to use as back-scratchers to relieve the most awkward of itches!

The other elephants soon stopped jeering at the young bull when they saw what an advantage a trunk was. Rather than admit that they had been wrong, one by one they would sneak off to the crocodile's pool and present their snouts for extension. They all considered the danger and discomfort of the operation worth it to gain the advantages of a marvelous, flexible trunk. No one knows what Crocodile thought of all these exhausting bouts, but one thing is certain – he still went hungry!

The Shangaan, to this day, will point out that all new born elephants take time to learn how to use their wobbly, hosepipe-like trunks. They suckle from their mothers and kneel to drink from pans with their mouths, just as their ancestors did before they learnt how to master the use of their versatile trunks.

Sitatunga and Elephant

(A story from the Bakongo of Northern Angola)
This story explains why Elephant is vegetarian.

Long, long ago Sitatunga went to Elephant and said, "It is now the dry season and we should be cutting down the scrub so our wives may plant as soon as the first rains come."

"Well," said Elephant, "I cannot come today, but you may as well proceed."

Sitatunga went and all that day he cut the bush and cleared the ground for planting. The next day he also worked alone.

On the third day Elephant called on Sitatunga and asked him to go to the plantation with him, but Sitatunga said he was sick and could not go, so Elephant went by himself. The next day Elephant called for Sitatunga, but he was not in. Elephant enquired where he had gone, but he only received a vague reply from Sitatunga's wife.

Every day Elephant called upon Sitatunga but he was either sick or out somewhere. Elephant had to do nearly all the work himself.

Later, when the wives had planted and the harvest had ripened, Sitatunga went to look at the fields. He was very happy to find so much planted and thought how pleased his friends would be if he invited them to a feast. So he called the antelopes and other beasts of the bush and they had a splendid feast.

By and by Elephant thought he would go and see how his crops were getting on. No sooner had he arrived than he exclaimed, "Hello, who has been feeding on my crops and eaten my corn? I will set a trap for them and catch the thieves!"

The next day the animals, led by Sitatunga, came again to the fields. Sitatunga warned them, saying, "Be careful, for Elephant will surely set a trap for us."

But Bushbuck became careless and fell into Elephant's trap.

"There!" said Sitatunga. "I told you to be careful. What shall we do? The others have all run away and left us and I am not strong enough to release you."

Then Elephant came and was pleased to have caught the thief. He took Bushbuck down and the frightened antelope pleaded, "Please sire, Sitatunga invited me to feast," he cried. "Do not kill me! Do not kill me!"

"How am I to catch Sitatunga?" asked Elephant. "No, I must kill you!" and so he killed Bushbuck and ate him.

When Sitatunga heard what Elephant had done he was greatly annoyed and declared that as Elephant was their chief, the animals were quite right to eat the food that he had provided for them. "Is it not the duty of the father to provide for his children?"

"Well, well, never mind, he will pay for this," thought Sitatunga. Sitatunga made a drum and beat it until all the animals came, as if to a dance. When they were assembled, he told them that they must take revenge on Elephant.

Elephant heard the drum and said to his wife, "Let us go to the dance!" But his wife said she would rather stay at home and did not go. Elephant went, but no sooner had he arrived than they all set upon him and killed him. When the beating of the drum ceased, Elephant's wife wondered why he did not return. Sitatunga sent her the head of her husband, skinned and cooked, as her part of the feast and not knowing that it was her husband's head, she ate it.

"Oh, the shame of it!" said Sitatunga, "You have eaten your husband's head!"

"Nay, sir, the shame rests with you, for you gave it to me to eat, after having murdered him!" said Elephant's wife and she wept and cursed Sitatunga.

Since that day no Elephant has ever eaten meat.

Tsuro and Grandfather Elephant – and Why Elephant has Such a Small Tail

(A Shona story)

Grandfather Elephant was very arrogant because he thought himself the most cunning of all the animals in the bush. Tsuro the Hare decided to teach him a lesson.

Tsuro knew that Elephant was greedy, so one day he paid a visit to Grandfather Elephant's home and asked him, "Would you like some nice, sweet young groundnuts, Grandfather? I know a garden where there are some, just ready and waiting to be dug up, and as the owner of the garden is an old woman, she will never be able to hurt you."

"I am indeed very fond of groundnuts", Grandfather Elephant admitted. "Do please show me this garden."

So Tsuro led and Grandfather Elephant followed and soon they arrived at the old woman's garden. When he saw the lovely patch of groundnuts, Elephant quickly began to dig them up and ate them greedily without offering any to Tsuro. Tsuro, meanwhile, got some strips of young bark and began tying Grandfather Elephant's tail to a stump of a tree which happened to be close by.

"What are you doing to my tail?" asked Grandfather Elephant, who was so busy eating that he did not bother to even look round.

"I am only picking the ticks off it," replied Tsuro.

When the tail was tied fast to the stump, Tsuro called out loudly, "Old woman! Old woman! Look who is stealing your groundnuts!"

The old woman came out, followed by her sons and their sons and half the men of the village. Seeing all the sticks and rocks and spears the men carried, Elephant dropped the groundnuts he was eating and tried to run away. But his tail was tied so tightly to the tree stump that he could not move and Elephant was beaten black and blue by the sticks and stones and cut sorely by the throwing spears. Hare stood nearby, splitting his sides with laughter!

"Wait till I catch you!" Grandfather Elephant yelled at Tsuro, between

blows. One particularly painful spear stab in his rump led to one tremendous pull and Grandfather Elephant got away, leaving the end of his tail behind tied to the stump.

Elephant chased Tsuro until it was dark, but by then Tsuro had crept to the safety of his lair. Grandfather Elephant went home to nurse his battered body and his poor, bleeding stump of a tail.

When Elephant had left and Tsuro was sure that the coast was clear, he crawled out of his lair and ran back to the old woman's garden. There he untied the broken piece of tail and took it home with him. Tsuro then set some snares and caught a couple of plump young guinea fowls and put them into a pot with wild herbs. He then cut up small pieces of Grandfather Elephant's tail and put them into the pot. While the stew was cooking, he went in search of Elephant.

When Grandfather Elephant caught sight of Tsuro, he began shouting with rage. "You! Yes, you Tsuro! What do you mean by tying my tail to a tree stump! Do you know I broke off a piece of it trying to escape?" And he turned around and showed Tsuro the raw, red stump. "If I had not torn off my tail, the villagers would have killed me!"

"Dear! Dear!" said Tsuro, shaking his head. "Surely you did not think I did that to you? I would not dream of behaving like that to a friend. I am sure you must have mistaken me for another hare – you know how much alike we all look!"

Tsuro looked so grieved that Grandfather Elephant began to think that he must have been mistaken. "Perhaps it was another hare", Elephant admitted. "Hares certainly do look alike."

"I will prove that I am your friend," Tsuro assured him, "I will invite you to a feast; I have a simply delicious guinea fowl stew for lunch today – young, tender, and cooked to perfection."

Guinea fowl stew was one of Grandfather Elephant's favorite dishes. As soon as Tsuro mentioned it, Elephant's mouth began to water. "All right, I will come," he said. Elephant got up and walked alongside Tsuro.

As they came nearer to Tsuro's home, the delicious smell of the stew wafted to meet them. Grandfather Elephant could hardly wait to begin his lunch. He picked the very largest leaf he could find to use as a plate, ran to the stew pot and ladled out the stew with a piece of bark. Elephant piled the

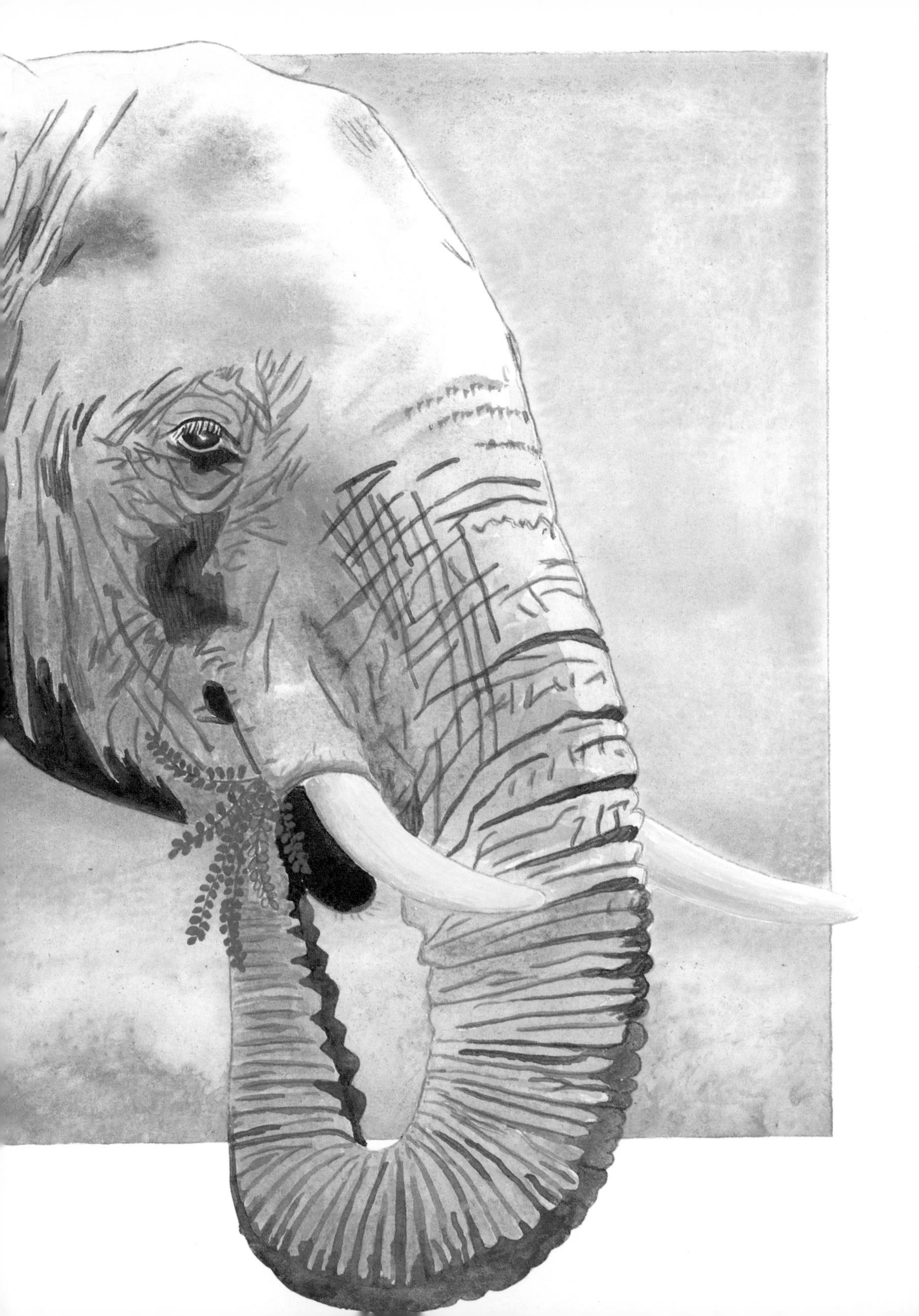

stew onto his leaf, not worrying to see if there was enough left for Tsuro, and began eating it, scalding his mouth in his greed.

"Ho! Ho!" giggled Tsuro behind Elephant's back. "Grandfather is eating his tail!"

"What are you saying?" asked Grandfather Elephant. He was making so much noise eating that he could not hear properly.

"I was saying that you have must have looked very handsome when you had a whole tail," replied Tsuro.

Grandfather Elephant went on gobbling the stew, and again Tsuro laughed behind his back and said, "Ho! Ho! Grandfather is eating his tail!"

"Did I hear you say that I am eating my tail?" shouted Grandfather Elephant. He looked inside the pot and sure enough, there was a small piece of his own tail floating in the rich, brown gravy.

Elephant jumped up with a howl of rage. He upset the pot so that the rest of the stew fell onto his legs and scalded him, but he was in too great a rage to notice. He chased Tsuro as fast as he could and as Tsuro slipped into his lair, Grandfather Elephant's trunk closed over one of Tsuro's hind paws.

"Ho! Ho!" laughed Tsuro down in the lair. "Grandfather thinks he has caught me, but it is only a root he has grabbed hold of! My foot is right next to it!"

Then Grandfather Elephant let go of Tsuro's paw thinking it was a root, and Tsuro climbed quickly further down out of reach. There Tsuro lay, curled up safe and sound and warm in his lair while Grandfather Elephant sat outside until it grew cold and dark and began to rain. Eventually he gave up waiting and went home to tell Grandmother Elephant how badly Tsuro had treated him.

To this day Elephant has never forgiven Tsuro for making him eat his own tail, nor has he eaten meat since. And to this day Elephant only has a small skinny tail with only a few straggly hairs at the end of it.

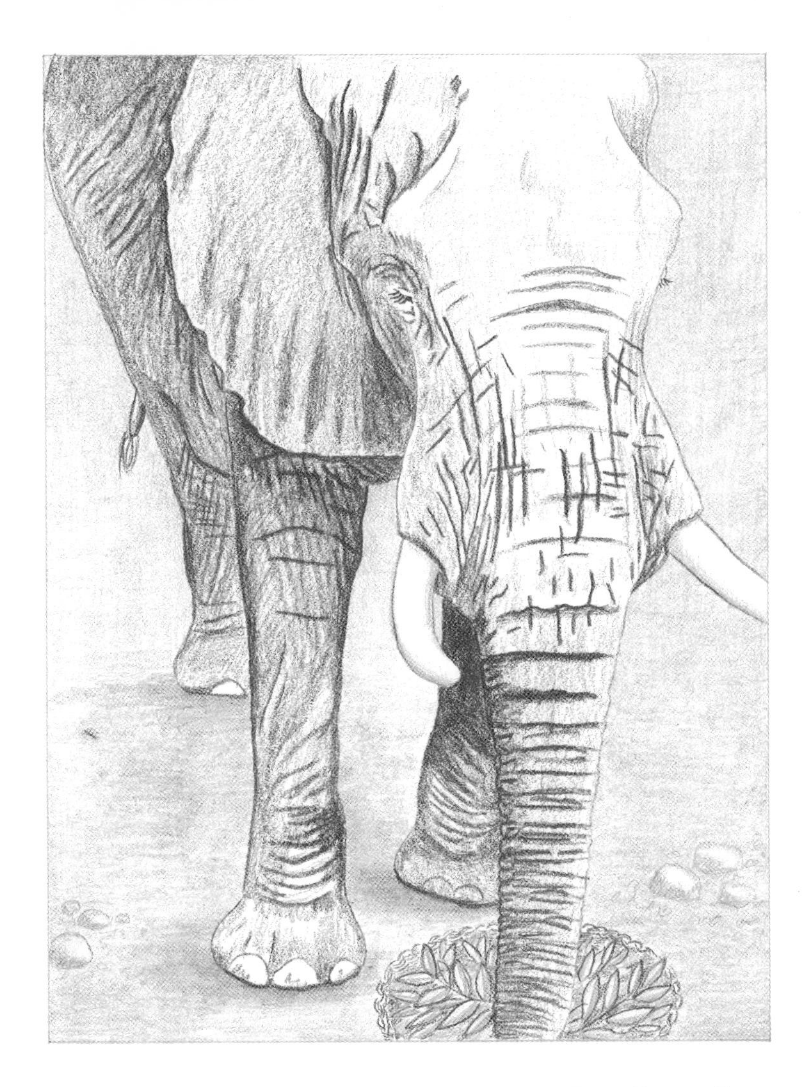

Leopard, Squirrel, and Elephant

(A story from the Efik-Ibibio of Nigeria)

Many years ago there was a great famine throughout the land and all the animals of the bush were starving. The bush was tinder dry and no crops or vegetation grew – even palm oil nuts failed to grow and ripen. Leopard, who lived entirely on meat, did not care for any of these things and, like the other animals began to get rather skinny.

However, in order to save himself the trouble of hunting, and since everyone was complaining about the famine, Leopard called a meeting of all the animals. He told them that he was very powerful, which they all knew, that he must have food, and that the famine did not affect him as he lived only on flesh. He told them that as there were plenty of animals about, he did not intend to starve.

Leopard then told all the animals present at the meeting that if they themselves did not wish to be killed, they must bring their grandmothers to him to eat, and that when the grandmothers were finished, he would feed off their mothers! The animals might bring their grandmothers in succession and he would take them in turn so that, as there were many different animals, it would probably be some time before their mothers were eaten. Besides by that time, he assured them, the famine would probably be over. But, in any case, Leopard warned them that he was determined to have sufficient food for himself, and if the grandmothers or mothers were not forthcoming, he would turn upon the young animals and kill and eat them.

The young generation who had attended the meeting had little liking for this arrangement. But in order to save their own skins they agreed to supply Leopard with his daily needs.

The first to appear with his aged grandmother was Squirrel. The grandmother was a poor, decrepit old thing with a mangy tail and Leopard swallowed her with one gulp and then looked around for more. In an angry voice Leopard grunted, "This is not the proper food for me. I must have more at once!"

Wild Cat pushed his grandmother in front of Leopard, but he snarled at her and said, "Take this nasty old thing away! I want some decent food!"

It was then the turn of Bushbuck and, after a great deal of hesitation, a wretchedly poor and thin old doe tottered forward and fell in front of Leopard who immediately dispatched her. Although the meal was very unsatisfactory, he declared that his appetite was appeased for the day.

The next day a few more animals presented their old grandmothers until at last it was the turn of Elephant. But Elephant was very cunning and he produced witnesses who claimed that his grandmother was dead so Leopard excused him, remembering that Elephant was longer-lived and therefore older than most.

A few days later all the animals' grandmothers had been eaten and it was the turn of the mothers to be sacrificed to supply food for the ravenous Leopard. Now although most of the young animals did not mind getting rid of their grandmothers, whom they had scarcely known, many of them had strong objections to providing their mothers as food for Leopard as they were very fond of them.

Among the strongest objectors were Squirrel and Elephant. Elephant thought about the dilemma – everyone knew his amiable mother was alive and the same excuse would not work a second time. He told his mother to climb a nearby mountain and he would provide her with food until the famine was over. He made her a large basket attached to a long length of stout lianas and instructed his mother to let down the basket every day so that he could place food in it for her. It was so strong that she could haul her son up whenever she needed company.

All went well for some days as Elephant used to go at daybreak to the bottom of the cliff where his mother now lived and place food in her basket. Then the old lady would pull up the basket and have her food, and Elephant would depart on his daily rounds in his usual leisurely manner.

Meanwhile, Leopard had to have his daily food. It was Squirrel's turn first after the grandmothers had been finished. As he was a poor, weak thing and not possessed of any cunning, Squirrel was forced to produce his mother for Leopard to eat. He was, however, very fond of his mother and after she had been eaten he remembered that Elephant had not produced his grandmother or his mother for Leopard's food. Squirrel decided to watch the movements of Elephant.

The very next morning, while Squirrel was gathering nuts, he saw Elephant walking very slowly through the bush. As Squirrel was high up in the trees and able to travel very fast, he had no difficulty in keeping Elephant in sight without being noticed himself. When Elephant arrived at the foot of the cliff where his mother was hiding, he placed the food in the basket and gave the rope a tug, after getting into the basket as well. He was hauled to the top of the mountain and after a time was let down again in the empty basket.

Squirrel watched all this and, as soon as Elephant had gone, he jumped from branch to branch of the trees and arrived at the place where Leopard was napping.

When Leopard woke up, Squirrel said, "You have eaten my grandmother and my mother, but Elephant has not provided any food for you. It is now his turn and I know that he has hidden his mother on top of a cliff."

On hearing this, Leopard was very angry and told Squirrel to lead him at once to where Elephant's mother was, but Squirrel said, "Elephant only goes at daybreak when his mother lets down her basket. Go early in the morning. She will pull you up and then you can kill her and eat her!"

Leopard agreed to this and the next morning Squirrel came to him as soon as Guinea Fowl announced the coming dawn. Squirrel led Leopard to the cliff where Elephant's mother was living. The old lady had already let down the basket for her daily supply of food. Leopard got into the basket and gave the line a tug. When he reached the top he found Elephant's mother and, as he could not bite through her thick hide, he threw her over the cliff. He could eat her broken body later when he had climbed down.

Shortly afterwards Elephant arrived at the cliff and, finding the basket on the ground, gave his usual tug, but there was no response. He then looked around and after a while came upon the broken body of his poor old mother who was by this time quite dead. Elephant knew at once that it was Leopard who had killed his mother and, since that day, Leopard has been his mortal enemy. Elephants also learned to live together in close family units, caring for each other and following the lead of the wise old matriarch.

"A debt is like an elephant's footprint."

A Nigerian proverb

When Frog was Braver than Elephant

(A Masai tale)

Once, long ago, Caterpillar entered Hare's lair when Hare was out. On his return Hare noticed strange marks on the ground and cried out, "Who is in my house?"

Caterpillar replied in a loud voice, "I am the warrior son of the 'Long One' whose anklets have become unfastened in the fight in the Kuritale country. I crush the rhinoceros to the earth and make cow's dung of the elephant! I am invincible!"

Hare ran away, thinking, "What can a small animal like myself do with a person who can trample Elephant under foot like cow's dung?"

On the road Hare met Jackal and asked him to return with Hare and talk with the ferocious warrior who had taken possession of his home. Jackal agreed and when they reached the place he barked loudly, saying, "Who is in the house of Hare, my friend?"

Caterpillar replied, "I am the warrior son of the 'Long One' whose anklets have become unfastened in the fight in the Kuritale country. I crush the rhinoceros to the earth and make cow's dung of the elephant! I am invincible!"

On hearing this Jackal said, "I can do nothing against such a man," and left.

Hare then fetched Leopard whom he begged to go and talk with the fearsome warrior in his home. Leopard, on reaching the spot, grunted, "Who is in the home of my friend, Hare?"

Caterpillar replied in the same manner as he had to Jackal and Leopard said, "If he crushes Elephant and Rhinoceros, he will do the same to me!"

Leopard left and Hare sought out Rhinoceros. The latter, on arriving at Hare's home, asked who was inside, but when he heard Caterpillar's reply, he said, "What! He can crush me to the earth! I had better go away then!"

Hare next tried Elephant and asked him to come to his assistance, but on

hearing what Caterpillar had to say, Elephant remarked that he had no wish to be trampled under foot like cow's dung. As Elephant was about to depart, Frog was passing by and Hare asked Frog if he could make the invincible warrior, who had conquered all the animals, leave his home. Frog went to the door and asked who was inside. He received the same reply as had been given to the others.

Instead of leaving, Frog went nearer and shouted, "I, who am strong and a leaper, have come! My legs are like iron and the creator has made me vile!"

When Caterpillar heard this he trembled and when he heard Frog approach, he cried out pitifully, "Please spare me, I beg of you, I am only a caterpillar!"

The animals who had collected nearby, seized and dragged Caterpillar out of Hare's lair. They all laughed at the trouble that Caterpillar had caused them and how Frog had been the only one brave enough to tackle the problem. Even Elephant had been too scared to help Hare!

King Elephant and the Waxen Horns

(A story from the Kikuyu of East Africa)

In the most ancient of times, all the animals in Africa were on friendly terms with one another. They made their own laws and rules and chose, from time to time, a king to rule them. At this particular time, Elephant ruled as the monarch and his subjects willingly carried out his commands.

One day Elephant was anxious to discuss a private matter of great importance that concerned a certain group of his subjects, the antelopes. So King Elephant called a meeting of all the horned animals of his kingdom, who prepared themselves for the meeting as soon as they heard the details.

Sunguru, the Hare, was not only upset, but greatly annoyed at being omitted from the summons, as he was, of course, hornless. But Hare is nothing, if not inquisitive, and the more he thought of the meeting, the more it worried him.

"I will attend the meeting!" he grumbled to himself and decided that by one means or another he would be there. However, not only would he have to deceive King Elephant, but also the antelope, into believing that he was one of their kind. It took a long time to come up with a suitable plan, but at

long last he sat up with a jerk and a large grin replaced the frown he had worn on his face.

Sunguru loped off into the nearby bush and made his way to an old antbear hole where he remembered there was an deserted beehive. He soon located it and carefully separated the wax from the honeycomb and, after a while he took a pile of wax back to his home. Then, with great skill and patience, he fashioned a pair of shiny, elegant horns. When he was happy with his work, he settled down for a night of contented sleep.

Early the following morning, Sunguru molded the magnificent horns securely onto his scalp between his little round ears. Off he went to the antelopes' meeting place, shaking his head from time to time to check that the horns held firm. Hare was very pleased with himself. "An excellent imitation," he smirked. "Those foolish antelope will never suspect that my horns are not real!"

When Hare had set off the morning was cool and pleasant, but the day was beginning to get hotter as he reached the meeting place. When he arrived he quickly mingled with the crowd of gathering antelope. He gave a sigh of relief for, thank goodness, none of the other animals recognized him. Even King Elephant's vigilant eye did not notice the deception. Hare was beside himself with glee as the meeting proceeded and he learned many of the private matters concerning the horned animals.

But as the day progressed, it became hotter and hotter. Hare was so engrossed in the events around him that he did not notice the wax horns were softening in the heat. Eventually he felt something trickle down the side of his face. Impatiently he brushed it away with his paw, thinking that it was perspiration until he saw, with horror, the melted wax on his paw.

He turned pale beneath his fur and tried to sneak away to hide, but others, too, had noticed his wilting horns. The antelope were too quick for him. He had not been the only one to realise what was happening and, seeing the tips of his horns beginning to bend with the heat, the antelopes cornered him as the false horns collapsed on either side of Sunguru's head. The jostling crowd caught and dragged him to King Elephant, shouting, "Imposter! Cheat! Spy!"

"Well!" said King Elephant, when he saw Hare's treachery. "If Sunguru wishes to wear ornaments on his head, I shall see to it that his wish is carried out, for they will act as a reminder of his deceit for all to plainly see!" King Elephant then ordered the horned creatures, each in turn, to pull the hare's ears with all their might.

The punishment was administered as King Elephant decreed, until Sunguru's little round ears had stretched and stretched and stretched to the length of the elegant waxen horns with which he had tried to deceive not only the antelopes, but his king as well.

To this day, Hare has worn his ears as the badge of his disgrace and he has been disliked and distrusted by all the horned animals around him.

Tortoise and How He Saved Elephant's Lands

(A Zulu story)

Once, long ago, the rains were very late and the countryside was parched and barren. Everyone's cattle were starved and thin, having to make do with licking the damp mud of the nearby river bed, for it was the only moisture to sustain them.

"The Spirit of the River is angry with us for some wrongdoing," muttered the elders as they sat in council. "Maybe an offering would appease the spirit so that he will once again bring forth water for our beasts and ourselves to drink."

Dinga, a young herd boy, overheard the elders at their council and at noon the next day, as his father's scrawny beasts licked the mud, he said,

"Oh, Spirit of the River, I will give you my father's best black ox today. He will be willingly given to you if you release the water for all to drink." Nothing happened.

"Maybe the red bull would please you more? Here is one, the best in all the land. Take the red bull and fill the pool for all to drink." Still no water was released from the river bed. In desperation Dinga offered Mhlope, the White One, his father's favorite milk cow – but the cracks in the hard, dry river bed seemed to widen in a smile at the refusal of his bribe.

"I have a little sister at my father's kraal. A laughing, fat and joyful child. I would even give her up if you would quench the thirst of all of us."

As he spoke these words the water bubbled up, cool and crystal clear, and soon the pool was full for all to drink. When his father's cattle had had their fill, Dinga drove them home. He then took his little sister, Nompofo, telling her that they would play beneath the shady trees that lined the river. After a while Nompofo fell into a deep, contented sleep and Dinga stole away, having fulfilled his bargain with the Spirit of the River.

When Nompofo awoke, she found herself alone and was scared. At this moment the Spirit of the River rose up out of the now running stream to claim his offering. Nompofo was so terrified at the sight of such a strange being that she screamed and ran as fast as her fat little legs would carry her.

She wandered through the hills for a long time, but was soon lost, straying

further from her home with each step. Finally, as night approached, she found a well kept field of mabele corn.

"Ah," she thought, "someone must live here." But she was wrong, for she had wandered far from her own chief's land into the adjoining Kingdom of the Animals. The field of corn belonged to Ndlovu, the elephant, King of the Animals.

Nompofo was hungry so she gathered some of the ripe mabele corn, made a fire, and cooked a filling meal. She then covered herself with branches and grass for warmth and fell asleep.

Early next morning Nompofo was woken by talking and laughing nearby. Peeping from her little hideout, she saw the elephant's animal servants collecting ripe mabele for their king's breakfast. Not long after she heard one of the animals say, "Alert! Alert! There is danger close at hand. Can you not smell a foreign scent in the air?"

All the animals put their noses in the air and sniffed. Then another one shouted, "A thief has stolen our lord Ndlovu's grain. See where the ripe fruit has been torn down!" They all stamped their feet in alarm and turned this way and that, but none of them could see the thief.

As they neared the thicket where Nompofo lay hidden, she blew her smouldering fire into a blaze and set the mabele field alight to drive the animals away. In panic the beasts fled before the flames to report the disaster to Ndlovu, calling out, "My lord, my lord, a thief is in your fields. My lord, my lord, your fields have been set ablaze!"

Ndlovu was very angry at being disturbed at such an early hour, especially as his servants had returned from the fields empty handed. No breakfast for the king! So Ndlovu called to Jackal, "You who sing to the moon, go and kill this creature who dares to spoil my crops!"

Unable to avoid a direct command, Mpungushe, the jackal, unwillingly returned to the field, dragging his tail along the ground and nervously looking over his shoulder.

On reaching the lands, he went from one thicket to the next, until finally he came to the bushes where Nompofo was hiding.

"I am Mpungushe," he called out nervously, "the bold and cunning Mpungushe. Come out and let me kill you!"

Nompofo made her voice as deep and fierce as she could and replied,

"Why should I fear one as insignificant as you? I am Nompofo! It is well-known that my horns are branched like a tree with ten sharp points to run you through. Ten of such as you would fit comfortably in my mouth. Get ready for I am coming for you!"

The jackal gave a piercing yelp and, with his bushy tail clamped firmly between his legs, bolted in terror back to Ndlovu's kraal without once glancing back.

"My lord, my lord!" he cried. "A wicked giant is in your lands. I saw him. He is taller than the trees. Even you, oh Mighty One, would be crushed beneath his foot!"

Silence fell on the animals as the elephant flapped his huge ears back and forth in obvious distress.

At last one animal spoke, "It would take more than a giant to crush my shell," boasted Fudu the tortoise. "I will rid you of your enemy!" Fudu swaggered down the path towards the lands; his show of bravery impressed all the animals at the gathering, even the mighty Ndlovu.

Nompofo was by now getting very scared and close to tears. Then she heard Fudu thudding down towards her, making as much noise and clatter as he possibly could with his heavy shell. Fudu sang loudly, "I am the son of my father. I am the son of my father!"

Nompofo could hide her fear no longer and ran screaming from her hiding place and made off into the forest. At this sight, Fudu stopped in his tracks and laughed and laughed and laughed.

At long last, he thought, Mpungushe the jackal had shown his true colors; the coward of the veld, frightened of a small child who had lost her way! Fudu decided, however, to keep this knowledge to himself so as not to belittle his own daring. He plodded back to Ndlovu's kraal, singing loudly all the while, "I am the son of my father. The mighty giant fled from the field at the sight of the brave and bold Fudu! I am truly the son of my father!"

There was great rejoicing in the kraal of Ndlovu at Fudu's victory over such a fearsome enemy. In his gratitude the elephant made tortoise his chief counsellor while Mpungushe was banished from the land for his cowardice. Since that day Jackal has never had the courage to hunt for himself, but follows the lion, contenting himself with the scraps Lion leaves behind and forever crying at the moon for his cruel fate!

Elephant, Hare, and Hippo

(A Shangaan story)

One day, long ago, Hare met Elephant and said, "Grandfather Elephant, great is your size, but I wager I could beat you in a test of strength!"

Elephant replied, "Who are you to challenge my strength? Could you even carry the weight of my leg?"

To this Hare replied, "I do not want to use my mouth in vain speech. Come, let me tie this rope to you and we will both pull, you towards the forest and I towards the river. I will surely beat you!"

Elephant was amused by Hare's overestimation of his prowess, but was willing to humor his wishes. It was time someone put an end to his vanity. So he allowed Hare to tie the rope round his hind leg and Hare laid the rope out carefully towards the river. Hare then went down to the river where he found Hippo and said, "Grandfather Hippo, I challenge your strength. Let me tie you with this rope of mine and afterwards tie myself to the other end and you pull into the river and I will pull towards the forest!"

Hippo laughed, just as Elephant had done, but Hare jibed, "You old Father Hippo, here is the rope; come let me tie you and prove my superior strength. When I shout 'Go' you must pull with all your might!"

Hippo, like Elephant, was amused by Hare's ridiculous delusion, but he went along with Hare's game, thinking that a good old soak in the river would bring Hare back to his senses. So Hippo allowed Hare to tie the rope around his hind leg and Hare then went to the middle of the rope and shouted, "Go!"

Elephant heard and Hippo heard – the first pulled towards the forest and the second pulled towards the river. Elephant was most surprised to feel the strength of his opponent for he did not doubt that he was competing against Hare. Taking the matter more seriously, Elephant began to overpower Hippo who was dragged out of the water and began to lament, "You have beaten me, you Hare!"

Elephant heard the noise and walked back towards the river and lo and behold he found he had been struggling, not with Hare, but with Hippo – an altogether different proposition!

"How is it that I am struggling against you?" asked Elephant incredulously. Hippo answered, "I, too, thought I was struggling against Hare."

Now they realised how Hare had tricked both of them and how he would make sure that all the animals of the bush knew that he had deceived them. They quickly united with each other and set off in search of Hare, intent on killing this tormenting upstart, but they were too late. Hare was long gone and had already started to boast of his latest mischief.

"When two elephants struggle, it is the grass that suffers."

A Swahili proverb

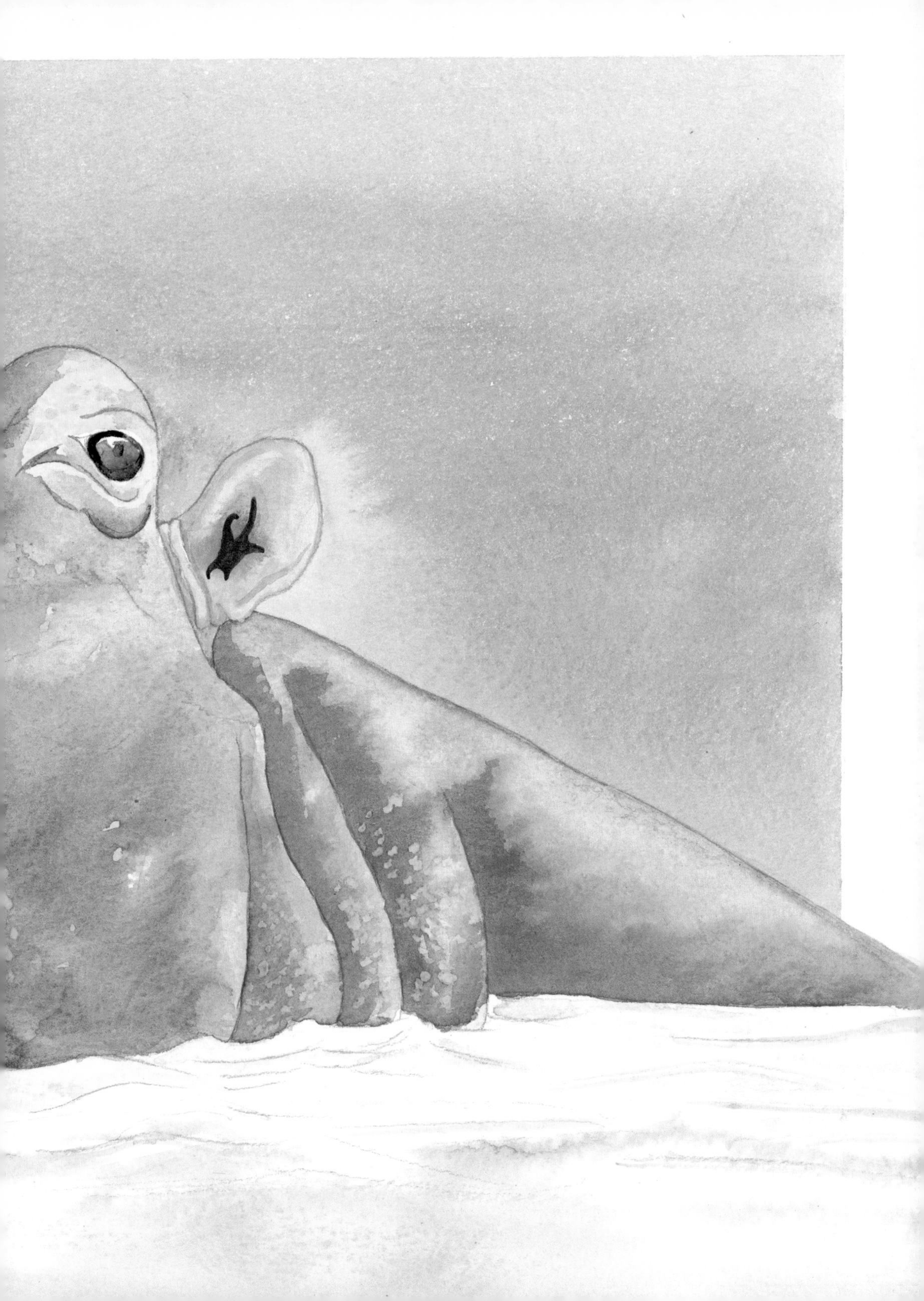

Elephant, Spider, and Hippopotamus

(A different version of the tug-of-war story from the Hausa of West Africa)

Once upon a time, long ago, there was a terrible famine. The crops had failed and there was no food to be had on either land and water. Spider and his family had finished their store of food and were beginning to feel the first pangs of starvation.

One day Spider went to see Elephant and said, "I wish you a long life. Sarkin Ruwa, the Hippopotamus, has asked me to visit you. He says that if you let him have one hundred baskets of corn now, he will give you a fine, black bull when harvest comes round. But Hippo insists that this agreement is to be just between the two of you great ones and that no one else must hear of it."

"Fair enough," replied Elephant and he gave orders for one hundred baskets of corn to be brought out. The young elephants picked them up and carried them to the water's edge.

"Put them down here," said Spider. "You have done more than your fair share of the work and can go home now. I will get Hippopotamus to send his youngsters to collect the corn. It will be quite alright here – no one else will take it."

As soon as the young elephants had gone, Spider called his family and together they carried the corn to their home and stored it away. The next morning Spider went to the river's edge and down into the water at the bottom of the river. He made his way to Hippopotamus' dwellings, passed all his subjects, and entered the private rooms. Here Spider bowed deeply to Hippopotamus and said, "I wish the Chief a long life."

"Well, Gizo, where have you come from and what brings you here?" asked Hippopotamus.

"I come to act as a go-between," said Spider. "Sarkin Tudu, the Elephant, has sent me with a message for you. He wishes me to tell you that he has plenty of corn for making meal, but has nothing tasty to eat with it. So he wants you to let him have one hundred baskets of fish now and when harvest time comes, he will give you a fine black bull."

"That seems a fair bargain!" said Hippopotamus.

"He also says that this is an agreement just between you two great ones," added Spider, "and that you must on no account tell anyone else about it."

"Alright," said Hippopotamus, and with that he gave orders for all one hundred baskets of fish to be collected. The young hippopotamuses brought them up to the river bank.

"You can go now," said Spider. "I will call the young elephants to collect them and take them to Elephant's home."

"But if we leave them here," said one of the young hippos, "what happens if somebody else comes and takes them?"

"Do not worry about that," said Spider. "No one will touch them here. But we simply can't have the young men of two different chiefs congregating in the same place. If you were to stay here until the young elephants turned up, goodness knows what bickering there would be between you. And then perhaps you would set your chiefs against each other.

"Truly," Spider continued, "they say it is young men who eat the beans, but the elders who get the bellyache!"

"That is true enough!" said the eldest of the young hippos. "We better go home."

When they had gone, Spider called his family again and together they picked up the fish and carried it home, dried it in the sun, and stored it away. Now Spider and his family had no more worries about food. From then until harvest time, Spider kept all his family busy plaiting a rope which was very, very long and very, very strong.

Then one day, after the harvest had been gathered and after the brush had been burnt in readiness for the next sowing, Elephant remembered the agreement and said, "Go and fetch Spider." And so Spider was brought in front of Elephant.

"Well, Gizo!" said Elephant. "Is Hippopotamus doing anything about the agreement you made between us?"

"I am sure that you need not worry," said Spider. "I will go right away and see him about it and be back the day after tomorrow."

So Spider went off and was away for three days. What he really did though was to go to the river bank where he marked out an enormous tree and tied the middle part of his rope around the trunk. Then he came back to Elephant, bringing with him one end of the rope and said, "Here is the tethering rope of the big, black bull which Hippopotamus is giving you. At daybreak tomorrow they will bring him out of the water and then as soon as you see the leaves of that tree over there shaking, your young elephants are to pull on the rope."

"So that is how it is to be," said Elephant.

"Yes!" said Spider.

After that, Spider went to see Hippopotamus, taking with him the other end of the rope.

"Elephant has given me a big, black bull to bring to you," he said, "but I am not strong enough to hold him so I have left him tied up to a tree on the bank. Here is the other end of the tethering rope. You had better send out your young hippos at daybreak to pull him in, but look out, for he is very wild and very strong."

"Alright," said Hippopotamus, "we will do that."

The next morning, Elephant had all his young males lined up holding the rope and ready to pull. As soon as the young hippos began to pull on the rope, the tree shook as if it was coming out by the roots and at that, all the young elephants began hauling as well. It went on like that all day with the elephants pulling at one end and the hippos pulling at the other end. If the

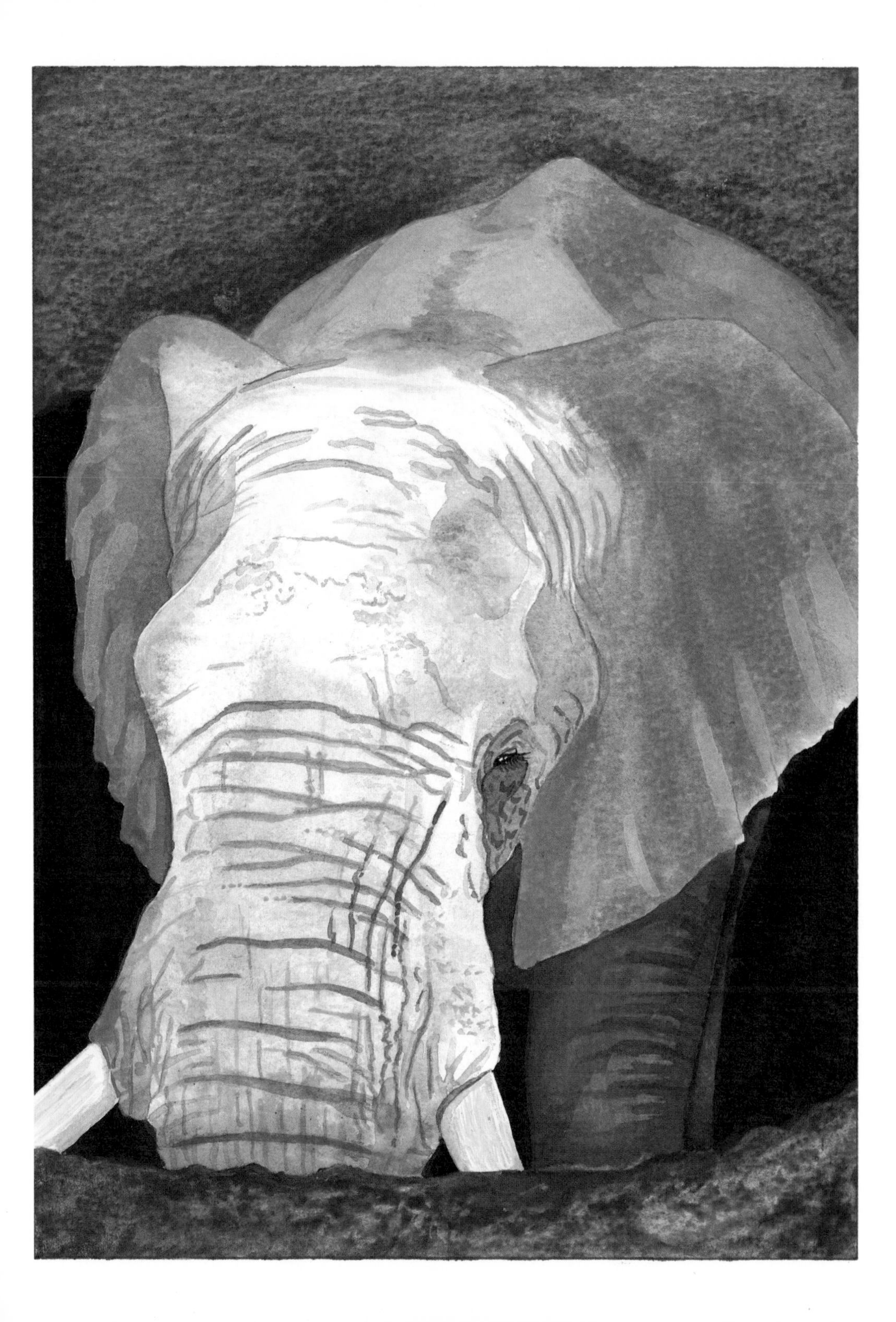

elephants gained any ground, the hippos pulled harder onto the rope and if the hippos gained any ground, the elephants did the same. They pulled and they tugged and they tugged and they pulled and it was not till nightfall that the two teams stopped to lie down and rest.

At daybreak the next morning, they all got up and started pulling again, the elephants at one end and the hippos at the other. Again the two teams tugged and hauled. At last, when it was midday, Hippopotamus told his young hippos to stop. "Go and ask Elephant," said their bewildered chief, "what kind of bull is this that he has given me?"

At the same time, Elephant was telling the young elephants to stop pulling and go and ask Hippopotamus what kind of bull he had given him. So both parties of young males set off and it so happened that they met up.

"Where are you all off to?" asked the young elephants.

"We have been sent to speak to the old Elephant," explained the young hippos, "and ask what kind of bull it is that he has given our chief in settlement for one hundred baskets of fish. We have been pulling on the creature's rope all day yesterday and since daybreak today, and we are utterly worn out!"

"But that is impossible!" exclaimed the young elephants. "We have been sent to speak to the old Hippopotamus to ask him what kind of bull it is that he has given our chief in settlement for the one hundred baskets of corn. He promised us a bull and we have been pulling at its rope all yesterday and since daybreak today, until there is no strength left in us!"

The two parties of youngsters argued like this for some time and things nearly came to blows. At last they realised that the old Elephant and the old Hippopotamus had not met when they had made the agreement, and that it was Spider who had been the go-between. They realised that it was Spider who had made away with the one hundred baskets of corn and the one hundred baskets of fish.

"Well, if that is how things are," they all decided, "we had better go back and tell our chiefs that there is no bull here and it looks like one of Spider's tricks!"

So both parties went back and told what had happened and what they guessed Spider had been up to.

"But I do not owe Hippopotamus anything," protested Elephant when he heard the news. "It is he who is in debt to me!"

"I am not in debt to Elephant," said Hippopotamus, "it is the other way round!"

But at last the old Elephant and the old Hippopotamus realised that Spider had tricked them and had taken all their food. Hippopotamus accordingly sent a message to Elephant to say that they must not be angry with each other.

"After all," Hippopotamus said, "we are among the great ones of the world and if we fall out, the quarrel will not easily be repaired. Instead it would be as well for us to lie in wait and catch Spider and teach him a lesson he will never forget for tricking us out of so much food!"

Elephant agreed with the wisdom of this and from then on both of them starting hunting for Spider. But neither Elephant nor Hippopotamus were able to find him anywhere because Spider was so good at hiding in many secret places. From that day on, Spider has grown quite thin as he is always hiding from the vengeance of Elephant and Hippopotamus!

"One who cannot pick up an ant but wants to pick up an elephant will someday see his folly."

A proverb from the Jabu tribe of West Africa

Elephant and the Wisdom of the World

(A story from the Yorubu of Southern Nigeria)

Once upon a time Elephant, who was very ambitious, thought that he would like to possess all the wisdom in the world and, as a result, become the only wise person in the whole world. If he succeeded in his ambition, he would be so wise that everybody, including great kings and aged councillors, would have to consult with him whenever they wanted to solve any problem, no matter how small or insignificant. Being greedy by nature, Elephant thought that he would charge people for these meetings and they would have to pay for his advice with armloads of food which would certainly make life easier for him.

So Elephant set out to collect all the wisdom he could find. As he gathered each piece, he put it into a large gourd, the opening of which he stoppered with a wad of rolled leaves. This took a long, long time and when Elephant thought he had collected all the wisdom, he decided to hide the gourd at the top of a very high tree which no one would be able to climb.

When Elephant got to the tree he tore off a strip of bark to make a rope to carry the gourd. Elephant put the loop around his neck and the gourd hung against his chest, between his front legs. Elephant then tried to climb the tree, but found it to be an impossible task. The harder he tried, the more the gourd got in the way and was in danger of being smashed.

His efforts to climb the tree were in vain. As he stood at its base wondering what to do next, he realised someone nearby was laughing heartily at him. Elephant turned round and saw a red colobus monkey watching him.

"Friend," said the monkey, "why don't you hang that gourd behind you if you want to get to the top of the tree?"

On hearing this piece of common sense advice, and realising that there was at least that much wisdom left in a world which he thought he had deprived of all wisdom, Elephant was so frustrated at the hopelessness of his task that he dropped the gourd of wisdom at the base of the tree. It broke and from thereafter the wisdom of the world was scattered in little pieces everywhere and so now anyone can find a little of it if they search hard enough. And maybe, if Elephant had used the wisdom he had gathered rather than tried to hide it away, he would have solved his predicament.

Elephant and the Devious Hare

(A story from the Wakamba of East Africa)

One day, long ago, Hare said to Elephant, "Let us meet in the big forest over there so that we may have a race and see who runs faster!"

Elephant agreed to this and left. Hare went to his wife and said, "Tomorrow you must be at the great tree in the middle of the forest and when Elephant arrives you must say to him, 'I reached the tree a long time ago. This is the finishing place.'"

The following morning Hare and Elephant met at the edge of the big forest and started running. Elephant pushed his way through the trees and dense undergrowth, but Hare just hopped here and there. After a while Hare went back to the starting place and hid himself.

Meanwhile Elephant reached the great tree where he found Hare's wife sitting there waiting for him. She greeted him and said, "Oh, my friend! I arrived here a long time ago. I have beaten you!"

"Never mind," answered Elephant, "let us now run back to where we started."

Off they went, but Hare's wife soon hid in the undergrowth while Elephant struggled on. When he arrived back at the starting point, there was Hare waiting for him. Hare said, "I have beaten you again, my friend!"

Elephant was disappointed at losing the race a second time and complained, saying "Why can I not run as fast as you?"

Hare replied, "Maybe it is on account of your fat buttocks!"

With that Elephant asked Hare to cut them off so that he could run really fast. After the operation, Elephant challenged Hare to one more race. They ran and this time Elephant beat Hare because Hare had not told his wife to wait at the big tree for a third race. This convinced Elephant who said, "I believe you, my friend, that my big bottom kept me from running fast."

But Elephant's wounds would not heal – on the contrary they got worse. So Elephant called on Leopard and said to him, "Go to Hare and tell him that I want my buttocks put back!" Leopard promptly went to Hare's home where he found him sitting outside and delivered the message. Hare said, "Our food is nearly ready; please stay and eat with us and after dinner you can go back to Elephant."

Leopard agreed willingly and ate his fill of the tasty meal. When they had finished Hare told Leopard that the meat that they had eaten was the elephant's buttocks. On hearing this Leopard thought better of returning to Elephant who would undoubtedly be very angry with this news.

To this day Elephant has remained without buttocks, and some say the loose skin on his back legs looks like baggy trousers.

Elephant is Outwitted by Jackal

(A story from the Angoni of Malawi)

Once, long ago, Elephant's wife was going through their food store and could find no honey, which was their favorite food back then. Suspicious that her husband, Njobvu, had been secretly raiding the store, she called him and told him to go to the forest and find more honey.

Elephant started to protest that he had other things to do, but decided that he had better allay her suspicions. "Just as you say, wife, I shall go this afternoon."

Later Elephant set off to a place he knew where the bees had made a hive in a great cleft in the rocks of a nearby mountain. It was a long, arduous walk through the forest over the foothills to the distant mountain, but the thought of more honey for him to eat made him feel hungry, so off he went.

The journey was hot and tiring, but Elephant found the hive and collected several large honeycombs packed with sweet, golden honey. He wrapped them in banana leaves and placed them in a large, woven reed bag which he placed on top of his head. Pleased with his hard-earned reward, Elephant set off back down the mountain and into the forest.

At the bottom of the mountain there lived a family of jackals. The youngest was called Nkhandwe, after his father, and he was a very cunning little jackal. Nkhandwe was also very greedy and there was very little that he would not eat. Above all he liked to eat fruit and honey, and of the two he preferred honey because it was more difficult to obtain.

That afternoon Jackal was sunning himself on the edge of the path that Elephant was using to climb down from the mountain. As Jackal was lying there wondering why figs must grow beyond his reach, Jackal saw Njobvu walking down the trail with a large reed bag on his head.

"What," wondered Jackal, "could possibly be in the bag on Elephant's head? Surely it must be food, but what could it be? Fruit, perhaps, or maybe even honey?" If only he could find out.

The little jackal crouched down with his head on his forepaws and thought and thought, and all the time he kept his eyes on Elephant, who was coming closer. Suddenly a smile spread across his cunning little face. The next moment he burst into tears and began sobbing his heart out, or at least appearing to do so.

"Goodness gracious, what is all this commotion?" exclaimed Elephant, as he went to see where the crying was coming from. "Why, whatever is the matter?" Njobvu asked when he saw the weeping jackal.

"Boo-hoo-hoo!" bawled the little jackal. "I am so miserable. My parents are dead and I am all alone in the world. There is no one to care for me! Boo-hoo-hoo!"

"You poor little creature!" said Njobvu with real concern and sympathy.

"My father was so wonderful!" said Nkhandwe. "He was so good to me. He would often let me ride on his back. Now there is no one to give me rides. Boo-hoo-hoo!" The little jackal's wails grew louder than ever.

"Would you like to ride on my back?" asked the kindly Elephant.

"I could never get up there," sobbed Nkhandwe.

"Oh, that is easy," said Njobvu. "I can pick you up with my trunk, like this, and up you go!" Elephant curled his trunk round the little jackal, lifted him high in the air, and set him down on top of his head, alongside the bag of honey.

"Ooh! My father could not have done that!" said Nkhandwe, sounding surprised and a bit more cheerful.

"No, I don't suppose he could have, and I bet he couldn't squirt water out of his trunk like I can. A trunk is a very useful thing to have." Njobvu liked to boast about his trunk and rambled on and on about all the things he could do with it.

The little jackal pretended to listen and would sometimes say, "Can you really?" and "Oh, how clever!" and even, "Well, fancy that!" But Nkhandwe wasn't really listening; he was scratching a hole in one corner of the bag of plaited reeds.

As he scratched and sniffed, he grew more certain that the bag contained a real treat of sweet, sticky honey. Eventually he scratched a hole through the corner, and through the banana leaves in which the honeycombs were wrapped, and the honey started to trickle out. Nkhandwe licked it up as fast as he could, but eventually he missed a few drops which spilt onto the still rambling elephant's trunk.

"Dear me," said Njobvu, "is that rain that I feel? Is it raining little jackal and are you getting wet?"

"No, no," sobbed the little jackal, "it is not raining, Njobvu. Perhaps it is my tears that you can feel. I am so unhappy that I cannot stop crying. I do not think that I will ever be happy again!" The little jackal feigned two more sobs and then carried on licking up the honey.

"You must try and be brave, little one," comforted Elephant.

"I am trying, Njobvu. But I cannot help but remember all the kind things my father used to do – how he used to find such lovely fig trees and let me stand on his neck and pick the figs. I don't suppose you could find a fig tree?"

"Why, yes, there is a fig tree not far from here," replied Njobvu. "Shall I take you there?"

"That would be k-kind," sobbed Jackal. "I think I shall feel happier if I c-could see a fig tree once again." This time the crafty little jackal was speaking the truth for the honey was nearly finished and he thought some figs would make a fine dessert.

"Very well," said Elephant and off he went to the fig tree he had seen earlier. It was a fine old tree, thickly covered with leaves and laden with ripe fruit. It had wide spreading branches that almost touched the ground. This was just the sort of tree that little Nkhandwe had hoped for.

"Oh!" Nkhandwe said with one last sob. "Thank you, Njobvu. This is indeed a fine tree. It is almost as fine as the trees my father used to find for me." With that the jackal crammed his mouth full of figs, swung into the tree under cover of the thick foliage, scuttled quickly to the ground, and scampered away as fast as he could.

"Are you enjoying yourself?" asked Elephant after a while, but there was no answer.

"Little Jackal, I can't stay here all day. I still have a long walk home and it will soon be getting dark. Do you not want me to carry you further?" There was not a sound, or even a rustle, from the underbrush.

"Well," thought Njobvu, "what a queer way to behave. But I really can't stay here any longer. I hope nothing has happened to the little fellow. Perhaps I should call out once more." Elephant made a loud trumpeting noise and called out loud, "Nkhandwe, Jackal! I am going home!"

The sound, faint as it was, reached the little jackal as he raced along, and he laughed to himself as he ran home. Honey, figs and a ride on Elephant's back – and all in one afternoon! What a story to tell his family when he got back. The young jackal was very pleased with his antics.

Njobvu was still puzzled by Jackal's disappearance, but resumed his long walk home.

Eventually Elephant reached home and was met by his eager wife. Njobvu removed the bag from his head and was surprised at how light it now felt.

"I hope you had a nice walk and have brought plenty of honey with you. You have been gone a long time, I must say!" said Elephant's wife. "While you were gone I had visitors, Nkhandwe, the Jackal and his wife."

As his wife's words sank in, Elephant stared at her in amazement. "Who did you say?" he queried. "Did you say Nkhandwe, the Jackal and his wife?"

"Why, yes, and they could talk of nothing but how clever their young son is."

Elephant groaned inwardly when it dawned on him that he had been totally duped. "That wicked little jackal," he said. "Look at my bag of honey!"

"Empty!" his wife screamed, "It's empty! What has happened to the honey?"

Protest his innocence as much as he could, Elephant could not get his wife to believe that he hadn't eaten the honey himself. So harsh was the scolding he got from his distrusting wife that Elephant never ate honey again. Nor did he ever trust the wily jackal again.

When Spider Saved Elephant

(A Zulu story)

In the beginning of time, Africa had many big areas of wilderness divided into many kingdoms and many different sovereigns ruled the animals of the wild. One such kingdom was ruled by Ndlovu, the elephant king. He was good and wise, and all his subjects looked up to him and admired him for his wisdom. They often praised his greatness far and wide.

The Nkawu, the vervet monkeys, who were chatterboxes and could not mind their own business, were constantly admonishing the animals of the adjoining kingdoms for their lack of law and order.

"You should have one of the clan of Ndlovu to rule you!" they would taunt, throwing rotten fruit at all who crossed the border into their kingdom. "When drought strikes he digs holes in the river beds with his clever, long trunk so that the water oozes up for all to drink. Great is the wisdom of Ndlovu!"

The Nkawu swung from the branches of the highest trees, chattering and laughing in such a carefree manner that the animals from the adjoining kingdom said, "That is a land of song and laughter. Surely the Nkawu speak the truth. Our lord was never so wise, for when the great drought struck, he was the first to starve and die. We have been leaderless for far too long.

"Let us send Nkalimeva, an evil baboon-like creature, to tempt Ndlovu to be our king. Who, but we, have the vast moba cane fields? It is well known that Ndlovu loves sweet things above all else. We will send Nkalimeva as our messenger with a dozen of our sweetest sticks to tempt him from his lands."

They searched the cane fields for their bribe and tied the cane up with creepers from the trees. They loaded up Nkalimeva with this bundle and sent him on his way.

It was the daily duty of Ndlovu's subjects to gather food for their king and bring it to his royal kraal. Green saplings from the trees, green bundles of juicy grass, and, when, in season, ripe fruit from the trees and bushes. All vied to bring their king the best choice of succulent food.

Now, as Nkalimeva traveled deeper with his load into Ndlovu's kingdom, he took two sticks from the bundle and scattered splinters and chips of the cane along the way. The animals that crossed his path smelled the luscious sweetness and gathered them up for their lord. Never had such magnificent food come their way before or to Ndlovu, who was very pleased.

"I'll have more of this sweetness," he said. "Go and find me more!"

But this time his subjects searched in vain and Nkalimeva watched his plan develop from a nearby hiding-place. When the animals returned empty-handed and Ndlovu grew impatient, Nkalimeva knew the time was ripe so he approached the royal kraal.

"My Lord Ndlovu," he purred, as his forehead touched the ground in humble greeting in front of royalty. "I bring you gifts from far away. Our lands are ripe, our food bins are full, and this sweetness lies rotting on the ground!"

As we all know, an elephant's greed is his failing. Ndlovu welcomed the stranger into his home and day by day Nkalimeva fed him and gave him cane, piece by piece, until the last sweet stick was gone. On that day, when his subjects brought their daily offerings, Elephant said roughly, "Your boughs and grass are stale and withered. Find me more of this luscious cane!"

This was just what Nkalimeva wanted and he interrupted, "Allow me to find your food today, my Lord. I can find you moba cane. Let your people rest!"

With sighs of relief Elephant's subjects went to their resting places in the shade of the trees to sleep, for their searching had made them weary. When they had all gone, Nkalimeva said to the king, "My Lord, over the hill beyond the river that bounds your kingdom are fields and more fields of the sweet moba cane. I can only carry a little at a time for you, but if you come with me, you can eat your fill daily."

This was too much for Ndlovu, so off he went.

When the evening came and all Ndlovu's subjects rose from their rest, they returned to the royal kraal to seek council and receive their orders for the next day. To their surprise they found that the royal hut was empty. Ndlovu had taken his sleeping mat, and both he and Nkalimeva had gone.

"Oh!" wailed the royal children. "While we played they left for the hills beyond the river to find the great moba fields."

"So that was Nkalimeva's game," Ndlovu's subjects cried, and all those who were fleet of foot set off in pursuit. In time they caught up with Nkalimeva and their king. Nkalimeva realised that his deception had been discovered and he fled in fear, but he was quickly overtaken by the fleet-footed buck. Left and right they charged him, attacking with sharp-pointed horns, and all his guile and nimbleness was required to dodge their fatal stabs. At last he gave them the slip and headed for the safety of a large, spreading tree.

"Send for Nkau to pull him out of the tree," his pursuers panted, but night was closing in on them so they settled down to guard him. They all stayed closely packed beneath the tree so that he would have to step on them and give them warning if he tried to escape. At first Nkalimeva threw small twigs and leaves down on the resting bucks to test their vigilance, but each time they sprang to their feet shouting, "He escapes! He escapes!" Finally he realised that they were too alert, so he settled down to sleep.

Now, there are some gray, social spiders of the Stegodyphus family that live in Africa. They form colonies with many hundreds of individuals, all sharing accommodation in a huge, gray matted web. It was in a tree occupied by one of these great colonies that Nkalimeva was sitting.

To pass away the time, the animals whispered and talked to each other of Nkalimeva's wickedness in trying to entice away their king. The small spiders listened and were angry, for though they were small, they, too, were

loyal subjects of Ndlovu.

Without a sound they crept out of their large, gray web and waited for Nkalimeva to fall asleep, which eventually he did. Then slowly, stealthily, and silently they bound him to the tree with their strong, silken strands of web. Round and round they traveled, thicker and thicker grew the bonds that held Nkalimeva, until he looked like a large, gray lump on the branch of the tree.

When daylight came, the bucks looked up and wondered how Nkalimeva could possibly have escaped from them for he was nowhere to be seen. Then, far away in the distance, they heard the faint trumpeting of their king, summoning them back to duty. Grateful for his return, they stretched their limbs and obeyed the call of their lord. Left in peace and quiet, the small gray spiders could now settle down to their own feast!

When Nkalimeva failed to return with Ndlovu, and they began to hear stories of how his subjects had battled so valiantly to save their lord, the other animals decided that trying to kidnap Ndlovu was not such a good plan after all. They decided to seek a leader with Ndlovu's wisdom from among the animals in their own kingdom.

And the wicked Nkalimeva was never seen among the living again, but the little social spiders were well fed and content!

Elephant the Deceiver

(A story from the Angoni of Malawi)

Once, long ago, a terrible drought gripped the land and the wild animals of the bush went hungry. One day Hare and Elephant were sitting down talking and complaining of aching empty bellies when Hare had an idea.

"Let us go to the Chief of Namadzi (which means 'by the water') for he possesses much land and he may give us food in return for a day's work."

"By all means," agreed Njobvu, the Elephant, "if you are sure of the reward of food."

So off the two friends went and the Chief, glad to use their labors, gave them some beans to cook as they worked. The work was hot and arduous as the Chief had given them a large plot of land to clear with hoes.

Hare worked harder than he had ever done in his life because he was so hungry and wanted his meal so badly. Njobvu did not work as hard and often stopped to complain of the heat. At one point Elephant wandered off into the bush and plucked some palm leaves which he placed over his head and back to act as shade to cool him off.

When Njobvu returned to the fields, Hare had finished clearing his patch of land, but Njobvu still had a lot of ground to clear.

"You have been quick," said Elephant enviously. "I am so tired I shall never be able to finish this!" he said, waving his trunk despondently over the weed strewn fields.

Kalulu, the Hare, sighed and looked longingly at the pot of beans simmering over the fire. "I suppose I shall have to help him," he murmured sadly to himself, but he called out quite cheerfully, "Don't worry! I'll give you a hand." Wearily Kalulu began to hoe again.

At last the whole task was completed and the two friends lay down their hoes and walked over to the beans. How good they smelt and how good they were going to taste, Hare thought, but just as he was about to help himself, Elephant said, "Wait a minute, old friend. You don't want to start without me, do you? I must just wash the sweat and grime off my body. Wait here and keep an eye on the beans while I go and bathe in the river."

"Very well, but don't be long because I am dreadfully hungry," sighed Kalulu, with tired resignation.

Elephant was already on his way down to the river. He searched the banks and dug out some lumps of red and white clay with his tusks, then daubed himself with his trunk. When he was finished he was impressed with his fearsome reflection.

Meanwhile, Kalulu was sitting by the beans, licking his lips in anticipation and wishing Elephant would hurry back. Suddenly a horrifying roar split the air and Hare saw a huge, terrifying creature charging down upon him. It came from the direction of the river and to the scared Hare it looked nearly as big as Elephant. Closer and closer it came until Hare gave one shriek of terror and fled.

It was some time before Hare could pluck up the courage to return to the cooking fire. Cautiously Kalulu crept up to the bean pot and, to his dismay, there was not a single bean left! Miserably, Kalulu sat down and it was not long before Njobvu returned from the river, clean and smiling to himself.

"Are the beans ready?" Elephant called out.

"Njobvu!" wailed Hare. "The most awful thing happened. While you were away a terrible monster came and scared me away and ate all the beans. There are none left for us!"

"A terrible monster?" snorted Elephant furiously. "I don't believe you! You are cheating me! You have eaten the beans yourself!"

"I haven't, indeed I haven't," protested the innocent Hare. "It really was a frightful monster!"

"Well," said Njobvu slowly, "I suppose I shall have to believe you. We can't have any more beans until tomorrow so we may as well look for somewhere to sleep. I shall be glad of a good sleep after all that hard work!"

Kalulu said nothing. He was still so hungry that he could not sleep, even after all the hard work he had done.

The next day the Chief gave Kalulu and Njobvu another task and some more beans in return. Again Hare worked hard and finished before Elephant, and again he had to help Njobvu finish his hoeing. Then, when they had completed the task, Njobvu went off to bathe just as he had done the previous day, and as Kalulu sat watching over the beans, the same fearsome monster appeared, scaring Kalulu away and eating up all the beans.

When Njobvu returned from the river, Kalulu told him what had happened and he was very angry indeed.

"I don't believe a word of it!" Njobvu screamed. "You have eaten the beans!"

"I haven't!" declared Kalulu, stamping his foot in indignant rage. "I am going to make a bow and some arrows. Then if the monster comes tomorrow I will kill it!" So Kalulu set off to find some suitable wood.

Later that evening Njobvu asked Kalulu if he had made his bow. Kalulu nodded. "Let me have a look at it as I am rather an authority on bows and I can tell you if you have made a good one," said Elephant.

"Hmm!" Njobvu continued, when Kalulu brought the bow for him to examine. "Not bad, not bad at all, but it is too thick here. Still, we can soon put that right!"

With a sharp flint Njobvu carefully pared away the wood in one central spot until it was very thin indeed. Then he handed the bow back to Hare.

"There you are, Kalulu," Elephant said, "that is a good bow now. If the monster comes tomorrow you should certainly kill it!"

The next day everything happened just as it had on the two previous days. When the monster appeared, Kalulu took his bow and fitted an arrow to the string. As soon as Kalulu drew the bow it snapped in two, just at the place where Elephant had pared the wood away. So for the third time Hare ran away in panic and the monster ate up all the beans.

"Any luck?" called out Njobvu on his return from the river after his bathe. "Did the monster come and did you kill it?"

"No," answered Kalulu curtly, "the bow broke."

Now Kalulu saw the smile on Elephant's face which made him wonder, especially when he noticed some red clay on Njobvu's tusk that he had not washed off. On the morning of the fourth day, Hare got up very early and made a new bow and hid it in the long grass near the place where the beans were to be cooked.

The day passed as usual, Hare working more quickly and harder than Elephant, but when the task was done, Elephant went off to bathe and Kalulu went quietly to fetch his new bow. Soon he heard the roar of the monster and as the hideous beast came nearer, Kalulu drew the bow, took careful aim, and loosed an arrow. With a bellow of pain and rage, the great beast fell with an arrow embedded in its rump.

"Oh! Oh! Oh!" it roared. "Kalulu, how could you do such a thing just for the sake of a few beans!"

"So it is you, Njobvu, who has tricked me each day and left me to go hungry!" said Hare in a voice cold with anger and bitter with contempt. "Call yourself a friend indeed!"

"It was only a joke, Kalulu. I was going to leave you some beans today. But now see what you have done! You have wounded me and I will surely die!" Njobvu burst into loud wails of self pity.

"Nonsense!" said Kalulu, pulling out the arrow none too gently. "Your wounded posterior is nothing. Go back to the river, wash it, and yourself clean, and never dare try your tricks on me again!"

Slowly Elephant struggled to his feet and hobbled away, ashamed of his deceitful actions in tricking his friend. Kalulu watched him go and then turned to the pot of beans. How good they looked, smelt, and tasted!

When Elephant was Tricked by Hare and Baboon

(A Masai story)

Long, long ago a hare lived close to the banks of a big river. One day he saw a herd of elephants crossing the mighty, swollen river. Hare shouted to the biggest elephant who was carrying a bag of honey, "Oh father, please carry me across for the current is far too strong for a small animal like me to cross alone!"

Elephant told Hare to clamber on his back and then he waded slowly across the mighty river. While they were crossing the river Hare could not resist the temptation to have just a taste of the delicious honey. But just a taste was not enough and Hare greedily gobbled down all the elephant's precious honey. As they neared the far bank Hare asked Elephant for some stones to throw at the birds.

Elephant passed up several trunk loads of river pebbles and Hare placed them inside the honey bag so Elephant would not notice the loss of his precious cargo.

Once clear of the river, Hare asked to be let down to the ground again. He thanked Elephant before scampering off. The elephants continued their journey and, when they reached their destination, the big elephant took down the honey bag from its 'safe' position and opened it, only to find it full of pebbles.

Elephant quickly realised he had been deceived by Hare in return for helping him. In a towering rage he set off to find Hare and teach him a lesson, once and for all! He eventually found Hare feeding near a termite mound, but when Hare saw an extremely enraged Elephant storming towards him he quickly bolted into the mound!

Elephant thrust his trunk down after him, intent on hauling him out to give him the beating of his life. Elephant's trunk groped around in the burrow and eventually grabbed hold of Hare's leg. Hare was horrified because he knew he was in for a beating and so he shouted out, "I think you have hold of a tree root!"

Elephant, unsuspecting, let go of Hare's leg and grabbed onto a tree root poking into Hare's bolt-hole. "Ow!" screamed Hare in feigned pain. "You have me, Father Elephant! Ow! You have broken me! You have broken me!"

Elephant was very encouraged by these calls, but pull and tug as much as he could, and despite the great strength of his bulk, he could not dislodge Hare – or at least what he thought to be Hare!

At last Elephant had to stop for a rest. Hare saw his chance to bolt from his hole and escape from Elephant, who was now really getting worked up into a terrible state.

Off he charged after Hare, who now realised the trouble he was in. Hare raced for Baboon's lair and burst in, much to the surprise of the troop of baboons who wanted to know what on earth was going on. Hare then told them that he was fleeing for his life to escape the wrath of a very, very big animal.

The baboons assured Hare that he would be safe with them and told him to rest in their lair. Elephant arrived shortly after and asked the baboon sentry if he knew the whereabouts of Hare. The baboons talked among themselves for a while and then the troop leader asked Elephant what he would give the baboons if they told him where Hare lay in hiding. Elephant told them he would give them anything they wanted if he learned of Hare's hiding-place.

To this, the baboon leader replied that their price would be a cupful of Elephant's blood. Elephant agreed, after seeing that the cup in question was very small. Baboon then shot an arrow into Elephant's neck and a small spurt of blood gushed into the cup.

After a while Elephant felt sure that the cup was full and asked the baboons if they had finished. But the crafty baboons had put a hole in the bottom of the cup and Elephant saw that it was still only half full. They jeered at Elephant, saying he was a coward!

Elephant told them to continue and to fill the cup. So Baboon continued to bleed Elephant, but still the cup would not fill. Eventually Elephant began to feel weak with exhaustion owing to lack of blood, and he fainted, collapsing in a heap on the ground. While Elephant was unconscious, Hare left the baboons' lair and made good his escape.

When eventually a weak and feeble Elephant came round several hours later, he realised that he had been tricked yet again. But Elephant's memory is long and he vowed that no matter how long it would take, he would get even with Hare and his wicked friend, Baboon, and never again would he let them take advantage of his good nature.

Why Elephant and Buffalo Fight

(A story from the Ibo of Nigeria)

Even in the earliest of times, Elephant and Buffalo were never good friends. The cause of their unfriendliness was that Elephant was always boasting about his strength to all the animals of the jungle. This made Buffalo ashamed of himself, for though he was a good fighter and feared neither man nor beast, all the other animals commented on Elephant's size and strength and never mentioned Buffalo's.

One day Buffalo decided that this dispute should be sorted out once and for all so he went to Lion, who ruled all the animals of the bush. It was decided that Lion should choose who was the strongest of the two. Elephant and Buffalo were to meet at an appointed place, where all the animals had gathered to witness this spectacle, and Lion could pass judgement.

Buffalo arrived early and set up position on a track leading to the clearing. He started to paw the ground and bellow, "Big One! Big One! Where are you?" But his calls were only answered by a bushbuck on his way to watch the contest.

"I am only a small antelope on my way to watch the fight. How should I know anything of the movements of the Big, Big One?" said the bushbuck.

Buffalo allowed Bushbuck to carry on his way and then started to scrape the ground and bellow challenges again. For some time Buffalo's challenges went unanswered, except for the sound of the small animals on their way to watch the contest which was soon to start. Eventually Buffalo heard Elephant trumpeting and could hear him getting nearer as he broke down trees and flattened bushes in his path.

When Elephant saw Buffalo standing his ground on the track, both charged one another and a tremendous fight commenced in which a lot of damage was done to the surrounding jungle. A colobus monkey watched the clash from high up in the branches. No other animals were there to witness the contest as they had all gathered at the clearing and were waiting with growing impatience for Elephant and Buffalo.

Colobus Monkey decided that he had better report what was going on to Lion, who would be none too pleased that his instructions were not being followed. So off he went, but in the way of all monkeys, he forgot what he was up to. By the time he reached Lion, who was now in a very bad mood because his command was being disobeyed, the monkey had completely forgotten his purpose.

"I wonder what on earth it was that I came to tell Lion?" Colobus Monkey

thought to himself, not wanting to get the rough end of Lion's temper. Just then, Lion remarked that Elephant and Buffalo should have arrived at the clearing by now.

"Ah! That reminds me," thought Colobus Monkey to himself. Bit by bit the chattering monkey explained to Lion that he had seen Elephant and Buffalo fighting in the jungle along the track leading north and that they were making a terrible commotion. When Lion heard this he was very, very angry and ran along the track to the scene of the fight.

When Lion arrived he found Elephant and Buffalo still fighting, though they had nearly fought themselves to a standstill. Each had used his horns and tusks to great effect, and both animals were covered in cuts and bruises and looking much the worse for wear.

Lion was furious at their disobedience and promptly set on each one in turn, sending them fleeing into the jungle. Lion decreed that as no one had seen the fight, neither Elephant nor Buffalo could claim to be the strongest. In fact, said Lion, he was to be proclaimed King of the Beasts for had he not sent both of them scurrying off like weak little duikers?

To this day the Ibo insist that whenever Elephant and Buffalo meet deep in the jungle, they continue to fight, each still trying to prove he is the strongest!

When Elephant Married a Nama Woman

(A Khoi San story)

It is said that in the earliest of times Elephant fell in love with a Nama woman and married her. After the marriage she went to live with the elephant's kinsfolk, but the ways of the elephant were very different from the ways of people and she soon became unhappy.

She sent a message to her brothers. They secretly came to visit her and she explained her problems to them. Fearing for their safety, she hid them in a nearby pile of firewood.

She then returned to Elephant's kraal and spoke to her blind mother-in-law, who did not like the fact that Nama woman was not of Elephant kin.

"Since I have married into this family, I beg of you, has the ram, the one-without-hair-at-the-knees, been slaughtered for me?"

The blind mother-in-law answered, "Why do you speak of things that are not done by your people and have never been spoken of before? Besides, I smell the smell of a Nama."

The Nama woman said to her mother-in-law, "Should I not anoint myself in the old way and sprinkle myself with incense as you do?" And the mother-

in-law answered, "Hum, my son's sweetheart says things that she used not to say." She was pleased that her daughter-in-law was starting to accept the ways of her husband's kin.

Just then Elephant, who had been away in the bush, returned home and was in an irritable mood. It was as if he had found that his wife's two brothers had come for her. Elephant rubbed himself against the house. The woman said to Elephant, trying to ease his distress, "What I did not do of old, I do now. Which day did you kill the ram for me and when did I sprinkle myself with incense?"

Thereupon Elephant's mother said to him, "Things which used not to be spoken about are spoken now; therefore give her what she asks for!"

So the ram was killed and the woman grilled it herself. That night she asked her mother-in-law, "How do you breathe when you sleep the sleep of life, and how do you breathe when you sleep the sleep of death?"

The mother-in-law answered, "Hum! This is an evening rich in conversation! When we breathe the sleep of death we breathe 'sui sui' and when we breathe the sleep of life we breathe 'choo awaba, choo awaba!'"

That night the woman prepared all her things while the others were sleeping. When they were snoring heavily in the 'sui sui' sleep she went to her brothers and said, "The elephants are sleeping the sleep of death – let us make ready!" So the two brothers got up and went out, and all the packing was done in silence. When they were ready to go, she went among her husband's flock, divided it, and left Elephant only a cow, a sheep, and a goat.

The woman then said to the cow, "If you do not desire my death, do not cry as though there was only one of you!" She said the same thing to the sheep and to the goat. The woman and her brothers moved off with all the flock.

Now the animals that had been left behind cried and cried noisily in the night and made as much noise as if they were all there. Indeed Elephant suspected nothing, but when he got up at daybreak he saw that his wife had taken everything. He grabbed a stick and said to his mother, "If I fall, the earth will resound with a thud." And he set off in pursuit of his deceitful wife and her brothers.

When they saw Elephant catching up to them they turned off the path, but soon found the way blocked by a huge rock. Thereupon the woman said, "We are people behind whom a big company of travelers follow, so Rock of our Forefathers, open up for us!" The rock parted and when all had passed through, it closed again.

Not long after Elephant reached the rock and called out, "Rock of my forefathers, open for me too!" The rock opened and when he entered, it closed in on him, trapping him. There Elephant died and the earth resounded with a thud. His mother at home said, "It has happened as my eldest son foretold. The earth has just resounded with a thud signaling his passing." And she wept.

Since that day the descendants of Elephant have shunned the human ways, preferring the freedom and dignity of roaming the open bush.

When Hare Stole Elephant's and Giraffes's Hard-earned Food

(A story from the Hausa of West Africa)

One day, long, long ago, Hare suggested to Elephant that they should do some farming together.

"You can clear the bush and I will burn the trees when you have pushed them over." Elephant agreed to this division of labor and began pushing over trees to clear the land.

Next Hare went to Giraffe and made a similar suggestion to him. "I will push over the trees," said Hare, "and you can burn them." Giraffe agreed to this division of labor and went and burnt all the trees which Elephant had already pushed over. Hare, of course, took care that neither Elephant nor Giraffe knew what the other was doing!

When the first rains fell, Hare went to see Elephant. "Giwa," Hare called, "you do the sowing and I will do the hoeing."

Later on Hare went to see Giraffe. "Rakumin Dawa," Hare called, "I have done the sowing and so now it is your turn to do the hoeing!"

Still later on, when the corn had ripened in the field, Hare went back to Elephant and said, "Now, Giwa, if you go and reap the corn, I shall go and gather it."

When Elephant had completed his task and done the reaping, Hare went back to Giraffe and said, "I have finished the reaping and now it is all ready for you to gather."

Finally, after all the hard work had been done, Hare went to see Elephant again. "Well, Giwa," Hare said, "the corn is all gathered and ready so let us bring it in tomorrow.

"There is just one thing I should warn you about," Hare continued. "I have heard that there is a creature called Giraffe who is going to try to take our crop away from us!"

"Who, or what, is Giraffe?" asked Elephant. "Well, never mind, for am I not big enough to cope with most things? We will deal with this Giraffe tomorrow. Goodnight for now."

Hare went straight from Elephant to Giraffe. "I say, Rakumin Dawa," he called, "I've just heard about a creature called Elephant and they say he is going to try to steal our corn!"

"Who or what is Elephant?" snorted Giraffe. "Don't worry about it now, we will deal with Elephant tomorrow. Goodnight to you, Hare."

The next morning Giraffe was up early and the first to arrive at the lands. Hare arrived a few moments later and Giraffe called, "Look here, Zomo, where is that Elephant you said was coming to steal the corn?"

"He will be here soon, no doubt," said Hare. "Look, there he is now," he called, as Elephant appeared. "Do you see him?"

"Where?" queried Giraffe. "Do you mean that creature over by the hill?"

"That is no hill," replied Hare, "that is Elephant!"

"Mercy on us!" exclaimed the terrified Giraffe. "I cannot take on such a monstrous beast!"

"Alright," said Hare, "if you can't, you had better go and hide. Lie down there, stretch your neck along the ground, and keep quite still."

Giraffe lost no time in doing as he was told and Hare went over to meet Elephant. "Hey, Zomo," said Elephant, "where is that Giraffe you said was going to take our corn?"

"He was here earlier, waiting for you," replied Hare, "but he went off for

a bathe. That is his knob-kerrie over there," Hare added, pointing to Giraffe's outstretched neck.

"Good grief!" said a now very nervous Elephant. "If that is his knob-kerrie, he is a bigger beast than I can tackle."

"Well, then Giwa," Hare said, "if you feel you cannot take him on, then you had better run off before he comes back!"

So off Elephant ran towards the east.

Hare then went back to Giraffe and said, "Elephant has gone over to the east, looking for you, Rakumin Dawa. You had better clear off while the going is good and before he comes back and finds you!" Giraffe immediately jumped up and galloped off to the west.

So in the end Hare was left with all the corn. He took it back to his home and for a long time after that he lived a life of leisure. That is until the corn eventually ran out and, by then, none of the other animals would help Hare, knowing all too well his cunning and deceitful nature.

Since that day Hare has lived a dangerous life, avoiding the wrath of Elephant and Giraffe, as well as the anger of people whose crops Hare now has to raid, having acquired a taste for corn and vegetables.

Ever since Hare's deceit, Elephant and Giraffe have decided that farming is a lot of effort for a very little return. Instead they survive by eating the bountiful vegetation of the bush, though Elephant sometimes gets a hankering for corn and will raid farmer's fields when the crops ripen, causing a great deal of damage and misery.

"The elephant is enquired about from those ahead."

A Zulu saying

Chameleon and Elephant

(A story from the Shona of Zimbabwe)

Long, long ago, two pretty sisters would go down to the nearby river to collect water and wash and bathe. Often they would wade across a shallow pool to a little island where they would rest and sing.

But one day the river rose in a terrible flood. Their mother was frantic.

"Save my daughters!" she wailed. "The river is still rising and will cover the island – they will surely drown. I will give them in marriage to anyone who can save them!"

Many young men waded into the fierce stream, but the current was too strong and they had to struggle to save themselves. Then along came the chameleon who proclaimed, "I can save them!"

"Go and take snuff! What do you think you can do?" scoffed the onlookers.

"Leave him alone," wailed the distraught mother, "only let him try if he wishes."

So the brave little chameleon cut two hollow reeds and tied them together in the shape of a cross and then stepped onto his strange looking raft. As we all know, Chameleon possesses a substantial amount of his own sorcery, so it was not surprising that the raft crossed the raging torrent safely and reached the island. There he found the two beautiful girls and decided that he would take up the mother's offer and marry the pair.

"Come on girls, hop onto my raft. You are coming home with me to be my wives!" The grateful girls giggled and obeyed. They were not averse to the offer as they thought Chameleon was a handsome fellow with his colorful changing coat, and despite his big, popping-out eyes. Obviously he was using his sorcery again.

There was great relief from the girls' mother and the assembled crowds when the frail little craft landed and the girls were safely on the bank. Only Elephant was upset. "To think of those two pretty girls being married to that ugly creature!" he trumpeted. "This cannot be! Out of my way there, all of you people and animals. I will take them away by force!"

And so he did. Poor Chameleon puffed himself out as much as he possibly could, but he was no match for Elephant's strength, even with his sorcery. Elephant soon made off with the two girls and Chameleon was left alone – no one came to his aid.

Nursing his wounded pride, Chameleon took the two reeds, and putting one end to his mouth and the other in the river, he drained all the water from the river and all the rivers in the country. When the people came to draw water there was nothing with which to fill their pots. They searched far and wide, but no water was to be found.

When told of their plight, Chameleon said, "Go to the ngangas. Find out why the water has left you."

This the people did and the diviners said, "The bones tell us that there is someone behind all this who has lost both of his wives. It is he who has swallowed up all the rivers."

The people then ran to the elephant and begged him to give Chameleon's wives back to him.

"Very well," said Elephant, "but we will trick the Ugly One. Go and fill up all your pots, cups and gourds as soon as the waters come back." The people agreed to his suggestion and Elephant returned the girls to Chameleon. At once the rivers flowed, the waters gushing back to fill the pools and streams. All the people rushed to fill their water containers and, as soon as they had done so, Elephant stole the girls back.

"I will teach you a lesson, Chameleon" he sneered. "You think you are so

clever. Now we have enough water we have no fear of you!"

But Chameleon took his two magic reeds and, singing a magic chant, drained all the rivers and streams a second time. This time he also drained all the pots, gourds, and water skins until not a drop of water was left. Then he sat quite silent.

Now the people were very frightened and they gathered around Chameleon. "Please, Chameleon, take back your wives and give us water."

"Oh no!" said Chameleon. "I am no longer interested in the maidens. Elephant can keep them. Go now, I am tired of you all. Was it not I who crossed the river; I who saved the girls; but Elephant took them from me and not one of you came to my aid."

"Here are gifts, Chameleon, take them!" pleaded the people.

"I do not want your gifts, just go away," retorted Chameleon.

And so the people ran to Elephant, angry and fearful. "It is all your fault. We are going to kill you!" screamed the people.

"No need for such threats, I shall speak to Chameleon myself," said Elephant, who was very worried and went to see him.

"Chameleon," Elephant pleaded, "here are your wives returned to you."

"I do not want them," said Chameleon.

"Here are your gifts, too," added Elephant, who was by now getting very anxious.

"I have no need for their gifts. Go away!" said Chameleon.

"If you do not bring back the water, the people will kill me," Elephant begged. "Have mercy!" Elephant wept and howled for a long time, saying, "I promise never to take your wives again, not for a single day, hour, or minute. If you do not give us back our water, all the people and animals will be dead by sunset!"

At last Chameleon, who had a good heart, relented and a rush of cool water filled the stream and the rivers, pots and water containers.

"Here are your wretched wives," said the defeated Elephant with bad grace, pushing the girls forward with his trunk. "Now that I look at them, I cannot see for the life of me why I thought them so attractive in the first place. They have faces as plain as cooking pots!" And with that he stomped crossly off into the distance.

As he left, Chameleon laughed and laughed and laughed!

Elephant and the Rain

(A San story)

Once, a long time ago, Quap, the Elephant, and Xanus, the Rain, decided to get married. At first everything went well, but eventually they quarreled. Elephant kept saying, "I am the strongest of all living things," while Rain kept saying, "All that lives, lives through me."

To convince his wife, who wore the rainbow as a girdle around her waist, that he was not just boasting, Elephant curled his trunk round a big mopani tree and pulled it from the ground, root and branch. Then Elephant trumpeted loudly.

Rain watched him for a while and wondered whether she should not stab him with her tongue of lightning. Then her eyes fell on the withering leaves of the mopani tree.

Elephant thought, "Aha! She is beginning to fear my great strength and my booming voice." Then he trumpeted louder then ever and called all the other animals to come and see how his wife trembled when he spoke to her. But she did not wait for the animals to arrive. She merely said to him, "That boasting mouth of yours will be the death of you yet. I will take my things and go to my own people."

Elephant pushed his ears forward, curled his trunk in the air, and said, "I don't care where you go. I shall find the water I need in the swamps and in bulbs and roots."

Rain did not reply. She merely waved her girdle over the land and disappeared, and with her she took all the moisture. Elephant said to himself, "Aha! How nice it will be to have peace and quiet all day long!"

Hunger soon sat heavily upon him and he started ripping off the sweet bark of a mopani tree. He chewed and chewed, but found no sap in the bark. Then he said to himself, "My throat has become dry from quarreling with a woman who cannot keep quiet," and he went down to the swamp.

At the swamp, Elephant found only deep cracks in the surface of the ground. He then went to the sand dunes to dig for water bulbs, but all the bulbs were dried out. A strong old elephant bull, he wandered hither and thither, but his throat became drier and drier.

He dug a hole under a shady tree and lay down. Elephant's skin started to shrink as a result of the dry air. His mouth opened wider and wider and his skin continued to shrink. Elephant started groaning when he heard the whistle of Xan-bib, the black-bellied korhaan which is a small member of the bustard family.

In a hoarse voice Elephant called to Xan-bib, saying, "Man-with-the-whistle, come here so that I can send you to my wife, Rain!"

Man-with-the-whistle came nearer and Elephant took a string of white beads from his neck and gave it to the Korhaan.

"Here, take it," Elephant said. "She made it for me and hung it round my neck. When she sees that you have it, she will know that I sent you. Tell her to come to me quickly!"

Korhaan really started whistling when he saw Elephant's plight and took the string of beads. Elephant's groans made him hurry and Korhaan ran for all he was worth. Eventually he reached Rain and said, "Look at this string of beads that you, yourself, hung round your husband's neck. He asks you to come to him immediately."

Rain replied, "I will not go!" And she rumbled so loudly that Man-with-the-whistle lost weight from sheer fright and ran back to Elephant.

"Elephant," Korhaan said, "I have been to your wife. She refuses to listen."

Elephant's trunk was by this time too slack to lash the Korhaan, therefore

he only groaned. "You are useless, you 'who becomes lighter too quickly when scared!' Get out of the way – downwind, I say!"

Just then Pied Crow came along to see whether there would be some carrion soon and said, "Nxaa, Nxaa – out, out impatience!" Elephant called to Crow, saying, "Take these beads, put them round your neck and go and tell my wife that I am dying of thirst!"

The Black One with the white beads round his neck went to Rain, perched himself on a branch of a tree, and said, "Nxaa... Nxaa... I have come to call on the Strong One's wife!"

Rain did not like this type of talk so she split the tree with lightning. Crow flew to another tree and repeated his story. Rain split that tree too, sending

bark flying. But Crow persisted, flying from tree to tree.

Eventually Rain began to get tired of putting out her tongue and she said, "I have always told him that his boastful mouth will kill him. Go now and tell him that I am coming!"

Crow hurried to Elephant who was in a very weak condition, and told him that Rain was coming. And there she was already, wrapped in a dark blanket. There was not even a rumble and suddenly the air filled with the smell of rain.

By now Elephant was too weak to lift his head and, as he lay in the hole, it poured with rain. Elephant drank and drank, but everything kept running out of him.

Some people who had taken shelter under a tree took pity on Elephant and made a big, grass plug and started plugging the leak. In those days Elephant did not yet have a tail. But as soon as he was filled up with water, the grass plug fell out. Then the people drove in a log. This plug stayed in place and the water filled out the Big One's skin again so that he was able to stand up.

Rain came nearer and said, "Now, have you learned your lesson? I always told you that a big mouth is of no use. If I had stayed away a little longer, everything would have been over for you." Elephant did not say a word.

Now Rain became very annoyed and said, "It is useless saying nothing now! From this day on that piece of wood will be your tail!"

Elephant bowed his head and Rain disappeared from this world for good, leaving behind a hollow in the mountain which was full of rainwater for Elephant and the other animals. Elephant learnt humility, but nearly at the cost of his life and at the cost of his wife. She never walked the earth again, her presence only being felt for a short time each year when life was returned to the veld by the most powerful force in the bush – rain.

When Elephant and Chameleon were Friends and How They Parted

(A tale from the Bakongo of Central Africa)

In ancient times, Chameleon and Elephant were friends – they had drunk together from the same bowl. Where one went, the other followed. What one had, the other shared. Now it is different. Each goes his separate way and when they meet they do not greet each other. If Chameleon sees Elephant coming, he goes into the tall grass or hides behind a tree. If Elephant encounters Chameleon, he ignores him.

Once, in the old days when they were still friends, Elephant said to Chameleon, "Let us go away from this place to another land. Food is difficult to find here. In that other place beyond the river, we will find all that we need to eat."

Chameleon said, "Yes, let us go."

They began their journey. They went beyond the river and crossed the grasslands. The distance was great and they walked and walked. Then they heard a man calling to them, "You! What are you doing here?"

Elephant and Chameleon replied, "We are walking together. We come from one place and we are going to another."

The man walked over to them and said, "I am a palm wine maker. Last night I hung twenty calabashes on my palm trees to catch juice for my wine, but this morning the calabashes are empty. Which one of you stole the juice?"

Chameleon replied, "No, we are not to blame."

The palm wine maker said, "One of you has stolen the juice from my calabashes. Must I beat you both for it?"

Elephant became fearful and said to the palm wine maker, "Chameleon there, he must have drunk the juice. See, it has made him sleepy, his eyes are only half open, and how slowly he walks. He is afraid he will fall down. His head, see how it moves from side to side. It is clear that he is drunk from the palm wine juice."

"Yes," said the palm wine maker, "who can deny it?"

He then struck Chameleon with a stick. He beat Chameleon until Chameleon was almost dead. When the palm wine maker had finished and left, Chameleon could hardly move his bruised body, but Elephant only laughed.

Chameleon said, "You are my friend. We drank from the same bowl. He beat me until I almost died. You did not help me, you only laughed!"

"Friend Chameleon," Elephant replied, "am I a match for a man? Yes, I laughed, but all the time I was suffering with you. I laughed only to hide my sorrow."

Chameleon said no more. They walked again and after they had covered a great distance, they saw smoke and fire. A man called to them, saying, "You! What are you doing here?"

They replied, "Only walking. We have come from one place and we are going to another."

The man came to where they stood and asked, "Which of you set fire to my trees and garden?"

Elephant spoke out quickly, saying, "We are not to blame; we have just arrived here."

The farmer said, "My corn has been scorched. My family's trees have been burned. You evil animals! Admit your crime!"

Chameleon said, "Indeed this is a crime. How can an honest being remain silent? Look at our hands and feet. If one of us has played with fire, they will

be black with soot. If one of us has done this evil thing, the mark of the soot will surely be seen."

"That is true," said the farmer. He looked first at Chameleon's skin, which was magical in that its color could change, and it appeared clean. Then he looked at Elephant, whose skin was a dark gray-black color.

"Here is the criminal," the farmer said and seized a big stick.

"No! No!" Elephant protested, "This has always been the color of my skin! This is the way it is with all of my kind!"

"Speak no more silly words!" the farmer said. "Your skin is the color of soot. It is you who has set my fields ablaze!"

He struck Elephant and beat him again and again. When the man went away, Elephant lay motionless and silent. Then, little by little, he began to move and his power of speech returned. Chameleon laughed.

"You are my friend," Elephant said, "but the man tried to kill me and you laughed. Go your way and I shall go mine!"

So Chameleon and Elephant parted. One went one way, the other went another. In the beginning they had been friends; they drank from the same bowl. But from that day on they had nothing to do with one another.

The Bakongo say it is always this way: a person who laughs at another person's misfortune can expect to be laughed at when he himself is in trouble.

Elephant, Hare, and the Drought

(A story from the Swahili of East Africa)

One year, long, long ago, the sun shone hotter than ever before. There was no rain and all the pools and rivers dried up. The animals gathered together, wondering what they should do.

Then the intelligent elephant, who has the largest brain, addressed them saying, "I know where we can dig for water, but you must all help me. We will start at once and each of you will take your turn digging. It is hard work, but it must be done."

All the animals did their share, one after the other. Except for Hare, who thought to himself, "I do not have to work. I can rely on my cunning to get my share of the water, if they find it!"

When he heard that the other animals had succeeded in digging a well and had actually struck water, he appeared on the scene, armed with two empty water gourds and a jar of honey.

Now Elephant knew very well that Hare would turn up sooner or later, but he did not want him to get any water. His rule was, "No work, no water!" So Elephant had left Giraffe in charge of the water hole.

When Hare arrived, Giraffe asked him what he was doing there. Hare said, "I have just collected some sweet water the Creator gave me."

Giraffe said, "Let me taste it!"

Hare said, "This is not a good place. Let us go somewhere where it is cool and shady."

Giraffe agreed to be led away. When they were under a tree Hare said, "Now lower your neck so that I can let you taste this divine water." Giraffe lowered his neck and Hare quickly threw a noose (which he had secured to a tree beforehand) over Giraffe's head. Giraffe was caught and Hare descended quickly into the well, filled his water gourds, and went home.

The next morning Elephant arrived to inspect the water hole and found Giraffe tied to a tree. "How did you get into that position?" he asked.

"Oh! Eh! I saw a beautiful she-giraffe who came along and I tied myself to this tree lest I should relinquish my post."

So Elephant dismissed Giraffe and appointed Buffalo as the night watchman. Buffalo was a little harder to mislead, so Hare gave him a small taste of the honey. Having tasted it, Buffalo bellowed, "Give me more!"

Then he agreed to be led away from his post. Hare said, "In order to enjoy this divine water better, you must look upwards and close your eyes. I can then pour it down your throat more easily and it will taste sweeter." Buffalo did as he was told and Hare was able to slip a noose over his horns and tie the other end to a tree. Then Hare took a bath, filled his water jug, and urinated in the water. (Only the most disrespectful would pollute the communal bathwater in this manner). Buffalo could not stop him, for the noose around his horns held him back.

The next morning Elephant came round and found Buffalo tied up. He noticed that the water was polluted. Elephant rebuked Buffalo, who invented an excuse like Giraffe's because he did not want to admit that he had been humiliated. After that Elephant put one animal after another in charge of the well, but each of them was deceived by Hare, tied up, and then blamed for the pollution of the water.

Elephant's last watchman was Lion, who certainly should have been strong and fearless enough to frighten Hare. But cunning knows no fear not even of Lion.

Hare told Lion when he arrived, "You have a pimple on your head!" And Lion said, "Scratch me!" That, of course, was fatal for Lion as Hare possessed magical powers. By scratching Lion he bewitched him and Lion fell sound asleep.

After that everything was easy for Hare. He slipped a noose around Lion's neck and fastened the other end to a tree. Hare then filled his water gourds at the well after which he bathed and finally defecated in the water, just to spoil the water for his fellow animals. Finally, to enjoy his victory completely, he went to Lion and woke him, saying, "Goodbye, old man, have to go now; sorry you can't come with me! Anyway, thanks for the water. See you around perhaps!"

Lion, roaring with indignation over so much cheek and contempt for his rank, wanted to jump at him, but the rope tightened painfully round his neck.

When Elephant arrived for his daily inspection, he found the water fouled and Lion tied up. "What happened?" Elephant asked.

Then Lion muttered, "Oh, eh! There was a lovely lioness, she came and fell in the water and when I saw her beauty I was so overwhelmed that I tied myself up...."

Elephant said, "You are as stupid as all the others. Now go away! Since you have all failed, I will now keep watch myself and see what happens!"

Lion trotted away with his tail between his legs. Towards evening Hare reappeared and found Elephant himself on duty. Unperturbed, Hare called out, "Hodi, hodi," and Elephant replied, "Karibu, come near!" Then Elephant asked, "What are you doing here?"

"I have just returned from my well which the Creator made for me," said Hare, "and in it there is delicious, divine water which is very sweet."

Elephant demanded to taste some of it. When he had tasted, he wanted it all, and said, "Let us exchange. I will give you some of my water if you will give me yours."

Hare refused, saying, "As you are our king, I will give it to you for nothing. Let us go and sit in the shade, where we can enjoy it in peace."

As soon as they were sitting under the trees Hare said, "Now, if you look upwards and shut your eyes, I will pour it down your throat and that will ensure your maximum enjoyment." Elephant was deceived by Hare's magical powers of persuasion. He raised his trunk upwards and closed his eyes. Hare had brought an iron chain for the purpose and he slipped this down over Elephant's trunk, tusks and ears. Then Hare went to the well, filled his jars, had a bath, and left his droppings behind in the water, just to spoil it for everybody else. He then went quietly on his way.

When the animals arrived the next day they found the water fouled and their great chief in chains. They asked Elephant, "How did you get chained up?"

Elephant answered, "Well, you see, I am a big animal. When I fall down I do not get up easily, so I decided to chain myself to this tree. I was feeling rather sleepy and I might have dozed off and rolled over."

But all the animals agreed, "It was the little hare who tricked us all. He made you sleepy by using witchcraft."

At that moment Tortoise appeared. He had at last caught up with the other animals. He said, "Tonight I will keep watch and prevent Hare from fetching water and getting away with it." All the animals laughed heartily and said, "You, Mr Slow! Do you think your brain works quicker than that of Hare who has outwitted us all? Do you really think you are more intelligent than Lion or even Elephant?"

But Tortoise showed quiet determination. "You might as well give me a chance," he said. "I am the only one who has not done a night watch yet and if you do not expect me to be more intelligent than yourselves, I could hardly be more stupid!"

Elephant said, "Alright, let him try. He might, after all, find a way. You never know how a tortoise may catch a hare. If there is no one with two eyes who can see, we have to call in a one-eyed man to look for us!" The animals bowed to the superior wisdom of Elephant and so Tortoise was appointed

watchman for the following night. The animals went home without any hope of having clean water the next morning.

Tortoise, who is at home in water, descended into the well, dived, and lay down on the bottom to wait. Soon Hare arrived and called,"Hodi! Hodi!" But there was no reply so Hare concluded that the other animals were defeated and the water-hole was his. He came out in the clearing and, seeing nobody, took a long bath.

But when he wanted to get out, he found that his leg was caught in a hole in the bottom of the well. He wanted to pull it out, but he could not as his foot was held more tightly in the 'hole' which was, in fact, Tortoise's mouth. Hare pulled and pulled, trying to scramble onto firm ground, but all his efforts were in vain. Tortoise held him as fast as if he was in a jaw-trap.

At dawn all the animals arrived, together with Elephant, and there to their unspeakable surprise, they found Hare himself, with one leg in the water. They pulled him out, but Tortoise did not let go, so they pulled Tortoise out as well.

Elephant admired and praised Tortoise for having caught the nimble Hare. Then Elephant said, "It is alright now, you may let him go, he can't escape."

Tortoise looked around the group of animals with his beady eyes and said, "If I let him go, you will let him go, too. But alright, as you wish!" Tortoise let Hare go free and walked slowly away.

At that Hare regained his composure and said, "Now, before you take any harsh or hasty measures, remember that I am too small to be killed; it is just not worth the effort. You see, all you have to do is tie me up and lay me down at the crossing of the game trails and leave me there for the night. The next morning I shall have transformed myself into a much larger animal and then you can kill me."

"Then we will kill you," said all the animals. They tied him up carefully with his own rope, put him down at the crossing of the game trails, and left him there for the night.

After nightfall, Hyena, the Hunter-by-night, found Hare lying trussed up by the path. Hyena asked Hare why he was there and Hare answered, "For an ox. You see, I told Elephant that I could eat a whole ox on my own and he said that I could not. So we made a bet and Elephant decided to tie me up because wants to see me eat the ox. Elephant will bring it here tomorrow morning."

Heyday the Hyena said, "I would like to have a whole ox. I could eat it on my own and I am sure you could not."

Hare said, "Alright, if you insist. I will give you your chance to try. All you have to do is to lie here and wait. Tomorrow morning Elephant will come with an ox, but he will be surprised to find you here instead of me. All you have to do is to convince him that you are indeed Hare and that you have only transformed yourself during the night." Heyday eagerly untied Hare's ropes and sat down to wait. As soon as Hare was free, he leapt away and vanished.

The next morning Elephant arrived with all the animals and when they found Hyena sitting there they asked him who he was. Hyena answered, "I am Hare; I have transformed myself during the night." As this statement tallied with what Hare had said he would do, the animals, even Elephant, believed Hyena to be Hare.

So Elephant ordered them all to bring firewood. He had it piled up near Hyena, who found this an encouraging sight, for he was sure that the next moment the ox would be brought and roasted for him. After this he would devour the whole ox in their presence.

But when the bonfire was quite high, the animals seized Heyday, put him on top of it, tied him there with the rope, and finally lit the fire. Hyena started howling and cried out, "No, I am not Hare! It is all a mistake! I want my ox. Hare said I could eat it; I only had to say I was him. It is the ox you want to roast, not me!"

Some of the animals thought Hare had gone mad, but the majority just called him a liar. "You are Hare and we are going to kill you!" they said.

When Hyena was burnt and dead, Hare appeared from behind a termite mound and cried triumphantly, "No! I am Hare. You have made a mistake!"

Then Hare was gone. All the animals, as well as Elephant, ran after him, but they never caught him. Tortoise did not run. He stayed where he was and said, "It takes a tortoise to catch a hare!"

Unanana and the Wicked One-tusked Elephant

(A Zulu fable)

Long ago, a young widow called Unanana lived alone with her two children. Life was hard for Unanana as she had to fend for herself and her beautiful young children, mostly without any help from family or friends. When she went out into the bush to search for firewood, her cousin looked after the children.

One day when Unanana was out collecting firewood, which was a laborious and tiring task, Baboon, then Impala, and then Leopard, passed by her hut. Each one proclaimed the beauty of Unanana's young children as they played happily near the entrance to the hut. So impressed were they by her children's beauty, that even Leopard would do them no harm.

The next animal to pass by the hut was Elephant, who was not so well endowed with compassion, probably because he only had one tusk and the loss of his precious ivory had soured his outlook on life. The wicked elephant took one look at the beautiful, happy children and then charged up to the hut. So fierce was his trumpeting and rush that Unanana's terrified cousin fled into the bush in fear of her life. The elephant with one tusk then greedily swallowed up the two small children.

Unanana was grief stricken on her return to find her children gone. When her embarrassed cousin told her what had happened, she fervently hoped

that her children were still alive inside the wicked elephant. Unanana took a bagful of food, armed herself with a knife, and followed the elephant's spoor until she met up with Baboon, Impala, and Leopard. They told her to go further along the track until she reached a place of tall trees and white stones.

True to their word, she found Elephant in this place of tall trees and white stones. On being accused by Unanana of swallowing her two beautiful children, Elephant lazily denied doing such a thing, but Unanana persisted in her accusation. The wicked Elephant became angry as he was not accustomed to such badgering, and grabbed Unanana with his trunk and swallowed her, too. This is just what Unanana had planned and much to her joy and relief, she found her two beautiful children deep down in Elephant's stomach, along with some goats and dogs.

Taking her sack of food, Unanana started to feed her children while the goats and dogs looked on ravenously. Scornfully Unanana told them to build a fire and to roast the meat of the elephant to satisfy their hunger, which they promptly did.

As the fire started to send flames licking higher and higher inside the wicked elephant, he started to groan louder and louder, until eventually he died. Unanana then took out her knife and cut a passage through the side of Elephant and freed everyone.

Unanana returned to her home with her beloved children and lived happily ever after. Since that day Elephant's descendants never ate people, but one is wise to keep clear of an Elephant with a lost or broken tusk, whose temper might not be that benign.

The Hunter and the Talking Elephant

(A story from the Bakongo of Central Africa)

Once, long ago, Elephant was walking near a village when he fell into a pit trap set by a hunter. The elephant could not escape. When the hunter came and saw that he had caught an elephant, he was delighted. He danced around the trap shouting, "Ah! Elephant! You have fallen into my trap! There it was, plain to see, yet you walked into it! It is stupidity that has brought you to this fate!"

Elephant answered him, saying, "It is stupidity that has brought me here. Cleverness will bring you here, too!"

The hunter said in surprise, "Why, the elephant talks! Who has ever caught a talking elephant before? Whoever heard of such a thing?"

He hurried to the village, calling out to the people, "I have caught an elephant that talks, I have caught an elephant that talks!" The people gathered around him and he said, "I set my pit trap at the edge of the forest. An elephant came and fell into it. I spoke to him, saying, 'Oh, but you are stupid!' and he replied to me!"

The people said to each other, "He lies! There is no such thing as an elephant that talks!"

"It is true that other elephants do not talk," the hunter said, "but this one speaks. Just as we are here talking together, so the Elephant and I had a conversation."

The people said, "This man lies! Elephants do not speak the language of men!"

The hunter said, "If I lie, I will move my house from the village. If he does not speak, I will live forever out there on the edge of the forest where I have set my traps."

The people said, "We shall remember your words. As you have spoken, so it shall be. Let us go."

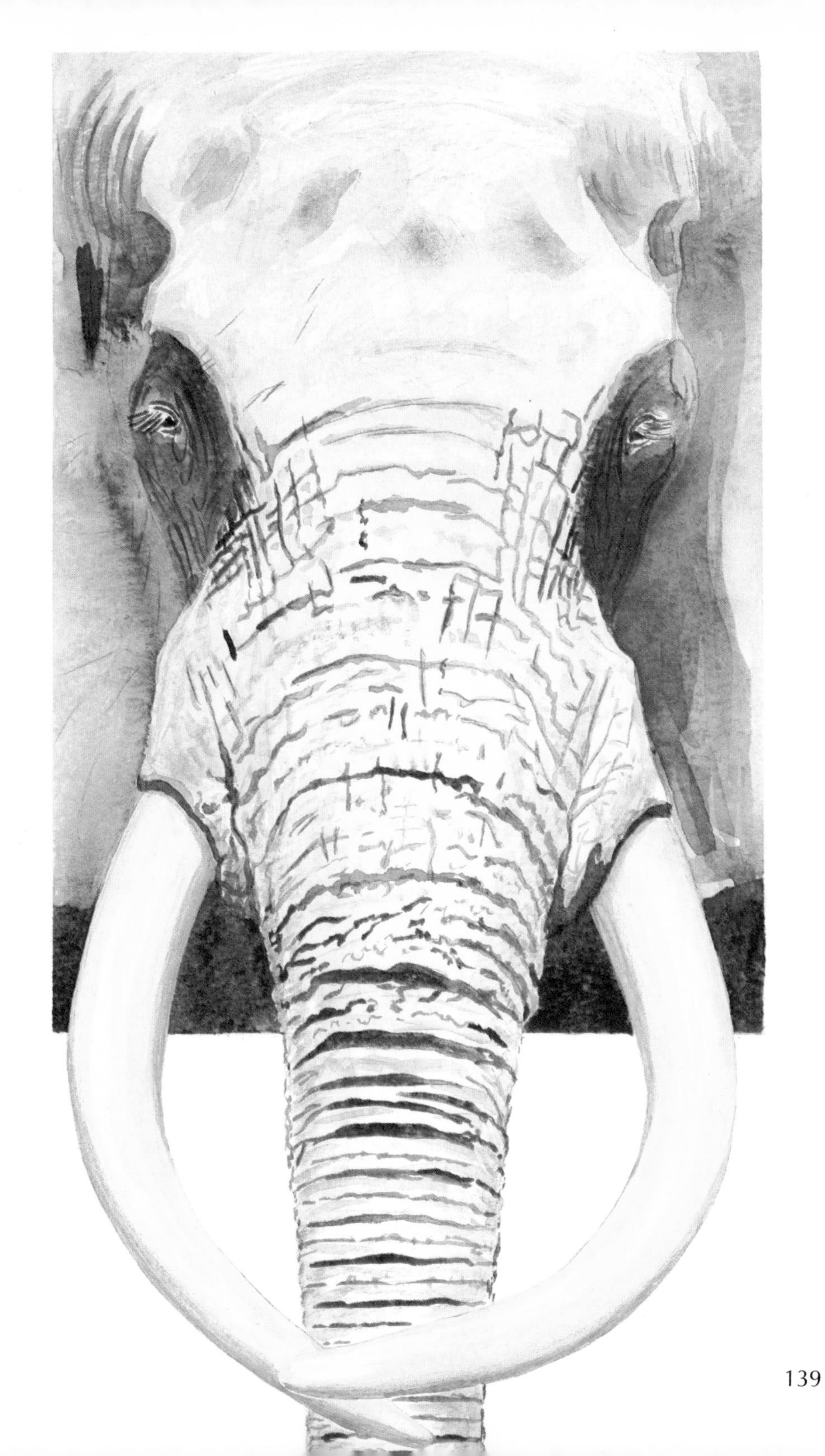

They went together in a crowd to where Elephant was caught in the trap. The hunter approached Elephant and said to him, "You who are caught in the trap, it is stupidity that brought you here!"

But Elephant did not reply. The hunter said again, "You, great one! Your stupidity brought you here!"

Elephant remained silent. The man prodded Elephant with his spear, saying once more, "You, Elephant, speak! It is stupidity that brought you here!" But Elephant said nothing.

After a while the people said, "Man, you lied! You said, 'the elephant speaks'. You said, 'if he does not speak, may I live forever in the forest instead of in the village'. These words you gave us from your own mouth; therefore do not return to the village. Build your house here." And the villagers went back to the village, leaving the hunter behind.

The hunter said to Elephant, "Oh, you foolish one! Why didn't you speak? You spoke before and when I brought witnesses you were speechless."

Elephant spoke then and said, "It is my stupidity that brought me here. You, it is your cleverness that brought you here. One of us was too foolish. The other was too clever. We end up in the same place!"

So it is said, "Too foolish and too clever, they are brothers."

Glossary

Adaptation — The process by which an organism becomes suited to its environment.

Baobab — A tree widely distributed throughout the drier, low-lying areas of sub-Sahara Africa. These long-leaved trees are distinctive because of their huge girth, smooth bark and Cream of Tartar seed pods.

Browser — An animal that eats mainly from the leaves, buds and twigs of trees and shrubs.

Bush A general term applied to areas of Southern Africa that still resemble their natural or original state.

Carnivore An animal that lives by eating the flesh of other animals.

CITES This stands for the Convention on International Trade in Endangered Species. CITES is a treaty signed in 1975 by many of the world's governments to try and regulate the huge trade in ivory, horns, skins, furs and other animal products taken from the wild.

Coppice A term used to mean the secondary regrowth of woody vegetation as it recovers from damage such as elephant feeding, bushfires or indiscriminate tree felling by humans.

Ecology The study of the relationship between living things and their environment, including both their non-living surroundings and other plants and animals.

Ecosystem The ecological system formed by the interaction of organisms and their environment.

Endanged A term applied to an animal that is threatened with extinction, usually due to pressure from people, either directly (from over-hunting or poaching) or indirectly (by changing the creature's habitat). Both cases apply to the African Elephant – poaching for the ivory trade and habitat destruction by the growing human population. The World Wildlife Fund's (WWF) "Red List" is a list of the animals most threatened with extinction.

Extinction When a species no longer exists in the wild or in captivity it is said to be "extinct". Extinction is for ever.

Fauna The animal life of a locality or region.

Flora The vegetation or plant life of a locality or region.

Forage The activity of grazers and browsers searching for their food.

Gestation Period The period of time required for a mammal to develop in its mother's womb from the date of conception, usually at mating, through to birth.

Grazer An animal that feeds primarily on grass.

Habitat — The immediate surroundings of a creature or plant that normally provides everything it requires to live.

Herbivore — An animal that feeds on plants.

Hunter-gatherer — A term applied to nomadic tribes, such as the San, or Bushman of Southern Africa, who live off the land, rather than relying on crops or livestock.

Indigenous — An animal or plant that is native to the locality.

Knob-kerrie — A short, heavy stick or club with a knob on one end.

Kopje — An Afrikaans name used throughout Southern Africa to describe a small hill or outcrop.

Kraal — An area surrounded by a stockade or fence, either for protecting livestock or a village.

Mammals — A term for the group of animals that are warm-blooded, have milk producing glands, are partly covered in hair and bear their young alive.

Muti — A Southern African term for traditional tribal medicines.

Nganga — A Southern African term for a person who knows about traditional tribal medicines and magic.

Omnivore — A creature that eats both meat and vegetation.

Pan — A natural water-hole.

Sanctuary — A safe place such as a National Park, where animals are supposed to be free from persecution and threat.

Savannah — Extensive areas of natural grassland.

Species — A term, singular or plural, for a group of animals or plants with common characteristics and which do not breed with others.

Territory — An area used by an animal for feeding and/or breeding, often defended against its own kind and sometimes defended against other species.

Veld — An Afrikaans word meaning open country or grassland.

Vlei An Afrikaans word used widely throughout Southern Africa for an area of marshy ground.

Wallow A mud or dust bath in which animals lie or roll in to cool off and obtain protection from skin parasites.

Weaning The state at which a young animal is no longer dependent on its mother's milk and starts to eat only the same food as the adults.

References

The African Elephant – Last Days of Eden, Boyd Norton, Swan Hill Press, 1991.

The African Elephant – Twilight in Eden, Roger L. Di Silvestro, National Audubon Society, John Wiley and Sons, Inc., 1991.

African Folktales and Sculpture, Paul Radin, Bollingen Foundation, 1952.

African Tales of Magic and Mystery, Maria Kosova & Vladislav Stanovsky, Hamlyn, 1970.

A Struggle for Survival – The Elephant Problem, Prof. John Hanks, C. Struik Publishers, 1979.

Bantu Heritage, H. P. Junod, Hortors Limited, 1938.

Elephants – Out of Space, Out of Time, Douglas H. Chadwick, *National Geographic* May, 1991.

Elephant Talk, Kathrine Payne, *National Geographic* August, 1989.

Elephants – The Vanishing Giants, Dan Freeman, Hamlyn, 1980.

Fireside Tales of the Hare and his Friends, Phyllis Savory, Howard Timmins, 1965.

Folklore of Southern Africa, A.C. Partridge, Purnell, 1973.

Folktales of All Nations, F.H. Lee, George C. Harrap and Co., 1931.

The King's Drum and Other African Stories, Harold Courlander, Rupert Hart-Davis, 1963.

Legendary Africa, Sue Fox, Everton Offset, 1977.

The Mammals of the Southern African Subregion, J.D. Skinner and R.H.N. Smithers, University of Pretoria, 1990.

Myths and Legends of Africa, Margaret Carey, Hamlyn, 1970.

Myths and Legends of Southern Africa, Penny Miller, T.V. Bulpin, 1979.

Myths and Legends of the Swahili, Jan Knappert, Heinemann Educational Books, 1970.

The Natural History of the African Elephant, Sylvia K. Sikes, Weidenfeld and Nicolson, 1971.

The Sacred Drum, Greta Bloomhill, Howard Timmins, 1960.

Sacred Elephant, Heathcote Williams, Jonathan Cape, 1989.

Specimens of Bushman Folklore, W.H.I. Bleek & L.C. LLoyd, George Allen & Co. Ltd., 1911.

When Hippo was Hairy and Other Tales from Africa, Nick Greaves, David Bateman Ltd, 1988.

Where the Leopard Passes, Geraldine Elliot, Routledge and Kegan Paul Ltd, 1949.

Zulu Fireside Tales, Phyllis Savory, Howard Timmins, 1961.